THE LINE

from Here to There

A STORYTELLER'S SCOTTISH WEST TEXAS

Rosanna Taylor Herndon

THE LINE

from Here to There

Texas Tech University Press

This book is typeset in Aries. The paper used in this book meets the minimum requirements of ANSI/NISO Z39.48-1992 (R1997). ∞

Designed by Barbara Werden

Library of Congress Cataloging-in-Publication Data
Herndon, Rosanna T.
The line from here to there : a storyteller's Scottish West Texas / Rosanna Taylor Herndon.
p. cm.
"Nationally award-winning storyteller recounts the Scottish West Texas experience over several generations through eighteen tales of extended family and friends. Topics include Texas tartans, seeing ghosts, the wagon trail, quilting, the sound of clocks, sandstorms, and the Davis Mountains"—Provided by publisher.
ISBN-13: 978-0-89672-630-7 (hardcover : alk. paper)
ISBN-10: 0-89672-630-4 (hardcover : alk. paper) 1. Scottish Americans—Texas, West—Social life and customs—Anecdotes. 2. Texas, West—Social life and customs—Anecdotes. 3. Ranch life—Texas, West—Anecdotes. 4. Herndon, Rosanna T.—Anecdotes. 5. Herndon, Rosanna T.—Family—Anecdotes. 6. Taylor family—Anecdotes. 7. Scottish Americans—Texas, West—Biography—Anecdotes. 8. Texas, West—Biography—Anecdotes. I. Title.
F395.S3H47 2008
976.4'0049163—dc22

2008001841

Printed in the United States of America
08 09 10 11 12 13 14 15 16 / 9 8 7 6 5 4 3 2 1

Texas Tech University Press | Box 41037 | Lubbock, Texas 79409-1037 USA
800.832.4042 | ttup@ttu.edu | www.ttup.ttu.edu

To my Scottish ancestors who came to West Texas
Their lives have shown me how
to work hard, give freely, laugh heartily,
and to double my efforts
when times are tough.

Contents

Preface ix

Storytelling and Academe: An Author's Note xi

Introduction 3
Texas Tartans 11
Sam and the Apples 18
The Line from Here to There 23
The Fugitive Doctor 30
Safe from Wolves 36
"Chocolate" 39
Safety Pins and Polka Dots 46
The Wagon Trail 54
The Sound of Clocks 56
Different Grandmothers 66
Seeing Ghosts 80
Panhandle's Coming! 83
The Song 89
Richard the Spy 97
A Company Christmas 105
The Boy 111
Balmorhea, Summer 1939 118
The Stonemason 126

Preface

I have been composing and telling stories to audiences for more than a quarter of a century. I was not a *writer* of anything except academic material, however, and most of it wasn't exactly heartwarming. In the mid-1990s the first audiotapes of my storytelling performances were released, and my daughter, Ceci Miller, a writer and book editor extraordinaire, kept saying, "Mom, you must write these stories down and do a book." When I protested she said, "Just write them the way you tell them." So, I did.

Somewhat timidly I asked a colleague, Dr. Robert Fink, to read a few of my efforts. At his urging I sent them to editor Judith Keeling at Texas Tech University Press. Her warm, gracious response surprised me, and I am grateful for her gentle encouragement and continued patience in waiting for this manuscript.

My daughter Ceci knows my voice so well that she sometimes recognized my intent in a story even before I acknowledged it to myself. She helped me polish many of these stories and acted as cheerleader when health problems interrupted my writing.

The early Scottish West Texans are the real reason for these stories—I wanted others to know them. Their unpretentious lives marked a clear path for me and for the generations to come. Old

Richard, our North Star, was the real family storyteller. His firm ethical stance, tempered with a playful sense of humor, still sustains us.

My son Richard, a fine storyteller himself, came to my aid to solve computer glitches, give business advice, and perform construction projects at home. His wise counsel and positive attitude are ongoing assets. My children and grandchildren made this project worthwhile.

A pioneer spirit lives on in many special people like my friend, Paula Windham, who generously allowed me to recreate her family's story of "The Fugitive Doctor" for this book. My late husband and best friend, Doyle "Peppy" Herndon, asked the questions that made me write the story of our childhood friend "Chocolate." I am also grateful to my longtime friends Chris and Edd Franks and Ann and Bill Rushing. They are quintessential West Texans who have been my strength in good times and bad.

My appreciation extends to my great storytelling base, the Tejas Storytelling Association, and to the Mesquite Storytellers of Abilene, the local guild that has courteously listened to my stories-in-progress.

Few professional women of my generation have been fortunate enough to have a woman as their mentor. Long ago a Baylor University professor, the late Chloe Armstrong, became my academic guide and kept me focused as a performer. She was a dear friend, and her impact on my lifework continues.

All of these people and many others played a role in the creation of this collection of stories. I owe each of them an enormous debt.

Storytelling and Academe

An Author's Note

STORYTELLING HAS LONG BEEN A PORTION OF THE ACADEMIC coursework for future elementary teachers and children's librarians. Until the 1970s the instruction and literature focused on telling stories to children. Scholars in several other academic areas recognized the relationship of oral narrative to their own fields. For example, specialists in oral language development had known for decades that children's first organized pattern of communication was narrative. As early as the 1940s, Edie Garvie of Scotland, working in multicultural and multilanguage education, understood that *story* could be a method for teaching everything about language. About the same time, students of oral communication began to connect their field with growing research in the behavioral sciences. A fusion of disciplines continued with discussion about where the study of storytelling belonged in higher education curriculum. Storytelling began to be recognized as an eclectic subject. It includes theory and application from the fields of literature and language, sociology, instructional methods, library science, creative dramatics, folklore, English composition and creative writing, philosophy, interpersonal and nonverbal communication, oral performance studies, psychology, and human relations. Now the academic study of storytelling represents a synthesis of research from the entire list.

When the storytelling renaissance was just beginning in the early 1970s, I was a delighted participant. The number of professional and semiprofessional storytellers increased rapidly. They came from varied backgrounds, but many of them seemed to come from theater performance or literary study of some kind. They were telling children's stories of all sorts and folkloric tales or Bible stories for adults. Only a few told true stories, and almost nobody told family or personal narratives. I decided I was a maverick among storytellers. Since I had a commitment to university teaching, I didn't even want to be a fulltime teller. I came to the storytelling community from a different direction. I had been a performer since I was a small child, but now I wanted to tell stories only about real people, especially people I knew. If I told another teller that, I got an astonished stare. I wasn't sure anyone would ever want to hear the stories I carried in my head. When they did, it surprised me.

I had been teaching oral performance of several types for years, but I didn't begin to teach storytelling until 1979. That year I started teaching an undergraduate storytelling course in a department of communication. There was no textbook for a course like mine. I used literature from six or more fields of study. Two years later I started teaching a graduate-level storytelling course. At that time, other colleges and universities were teaching storytelling with an emphasis in folklore or public performance. Those and other approaches have proven productive; however, a few colleagues and I considered storytelling a practical form of interpersonal *and* public communication. Researchers in interpersonal communication had begun to study conversation, and that gave narrative exchange new importance. Related topics like novelty and commonality of content emerged as compelling factors in listening. My students were encouraged to tell true stories as part of their repertoire. To their surprise, many found their well-constructed family narratives to be more meaningful to audiences than any others they told. When those stories ended, audience members came to the teller with their own stories, and insightful audience discussions about a story's topic were frequent. My students' family tales had touched their listeners' hearts, and the students wanted to know *why*. I prodded a little. Their integrated education was beginning. Some students began to discover the interrelationship among subject areas for the first time. Soon they were exploring literature in other fields on topics like empathy, imagery, cognition, and even the communication of time and space. The list was long, and they began to say, "Telling true stories relates to almost everything, doesn't it?" I celebrated. One day as I entered the faculty lounge, a philosophy professor said, "Rosy, I don't know what you are teaching this semester, but you have students reading in *my field*. Two of them hunted me down to talk about perception." A psychology professor chimed in, "One of your kids raised questions about self-perception last week that just amazed me. What are you doing to them?" I just shrugged and grinned, "Oh, they're just learning about storytelling."

Storytelling can be taught as an avenue into creative writing, public address, and other important areas. While I acknowledge all of those uses, my own academic background is in oral human communication, and my love of storytelling springs from that study. I am certain that powerful narratives emerge when they are coupled with insight into human behavior and the ability to think well. Everything else about storytelling is the honest and effective application of a set of skills and techniques. I have spent much of my career teaching those skills, but my main goal has always been to help my students learn to think and, hopefully, develop greater insight into human behavior.

To my delight, family and personal narratives gained new interest in 1976. The U.S. bicentennial and the Smithsonian Institution's oral history project brought the change. Suddenly genealogists wanted to learn to tell their families' histories with more than pedigrees. They were discovering that to make a family history come to life and be remembered, the *stories* must be told. I began to teach workshops for genealogy societies and storytelling organizations. Even now, research-grounded theory has not caught up with current instruction in storytelling, but a growing body of research has come from almost every field that is connected to storytelling. By 1980 a group of us were reading papers about the academic study of storytelling at Texas Speech Communication Association meetings. In 1984 I presented my first research paper related to family storytelling at a national meeting of the Speech Communication Association. That ongoing project was soon divided into two new studies: "The Impact of Family Stories on Concepts of Self and Family" and "Acquired Performance Mastery through Family Storytelling." No doubt graduate students will pursue that trend with more research. There are studies related to family communication in several disciplines. Many of them have implications for further study concerning family narratives.

Now there is a large community of professional storytellers in the United States, and nearly all of them include some family narratives in their repertoire. Every fall, The National Storytelling Festival brings several thousand listeners and eighteen or more of the best tellers in the country to Jonesborough, Tennessee. Many family narratives are told at that event every year. A number of colleges and universities teach undergraduate and graduate courses in storytelling. Several offer complete master's degrees in storytelling. We are still exploring the multifaceted place of oral family narrative in academics.

THE LINE

from Here to There

Introduction

In most families there is at least one storyteller who shares personal and family history. This was the case in my family. I grew up listening to my dad tell those stories and was fascinated by them. I was determined to remember every detail, especially the ripples of humor that ran through even the most serious tales. A solitary child, I retold the stories to myself in private, performing for my teddy bear and dolls until the words were indelibly fixed in my memory. It would be many years before I told them to a real audience.

Despite the fact that I had been urged onto the stage at the age of three (a reluctant performer of recitations, drama, song, and dance), I never in all those years considered the family stories as performance material. Not until the 1970s, when I became involved in the storytelling renaissance, did it occur to me that I might tell my family stories from the stage.

My family elders handed down their Scottish ways by example with little comment. Informed by their Scottish heritage, they exhibited traits now thought of as typical characteristics of early West Texans. (A further discussion of this topic can be found in T. R. Fehrenbach's *Lone Star: A History of Texas and the Texans.*) Those hardworking people were fiercely independent and self-reliant. I saw how tough and resourceful they were in times of adversity. Their speech was generally blunt to match their unromantic view of the world. They brought such humor to some occasions, however, that it added balance to the plain lifestyle they imposed. Their children were expected to think clearly in an emergency and focus on the problem at hand. (The title story tells of nine-year-old Nollie's extraordinary action in a life-threatening situation.) When they saw a wrong, they considered it their responsibility to correct it. (See "Richard the Spy.") I thought they learned that as part of the early West Texas culture. In fantasy, I pictured one of my great uncles in the middle of the street with a revolver in his hand like a western movie hero, although I knew that was never his style. Now I know their tendency to swift action came from a much older tradition they had learned from their elders. As a young adult I began to appreciate how uniquely peculiar and truly wonderful these people were. That fascination, together with the legacy of my dad's well-crafted tales, inspired me to do some genealogical research. As I made my way through several generations of family history, I was amazed to discover how accurate my father's retellings had been. In the genealogical society, other researchers told me that a typical family has only one member in each generation who learns the family stories. If that person fails to share the stories, they said, then in only a generation or two the stories will disappear, effectively erasing the family's history.

I knew that in the generation ahead of me, my father had been that crucial storyteller. Cousins and other family members often came to him, as I did, with questions about the family's past and about why our Scottish ancestors had migrated to the harsh terrain and climate of West Texas. But who would be the next generation's keeper of the family stories—stories I had privately rehearsed as my own treasures? I had not even shared them with my own children, who were then almost grown. With some sense of urgency, I began to tell the stories.

I put the family stories into a clear historic perspective when I took a course called Westward Movement in American History as an undergraduate. At that time I had just begun to understand that my Texas family was almost entirely Scottish. Years later in Scotland I studied that country's long and eventful history. With so much to learn, the migrations to Ulster and America were only a minor part of the material. I wanted to know more about the transitional moves my ancestors made after leaving Scotland and before arriving in West Texas. Tracing those paths was a tedious task. I learned that the Scottish immigration to the New World began even before 1717 and the period called the Great Migration. It continued for many years until the Scots outnumbered all other nations' settlers except the English. Now it is estimated that while Scotland's population is slightly over five million, there are some fifty million Americans of Scottish descent. Their migration was almost unnoticed partly because they shared a common language with the settlers from England. Most Scots had been speakers of English for centuries, and their tall stature and fair skin was not distinctive enough to set them apart. Unlike some other national groups, they did not create tightly knit towns that gave them a separate identity. They developed scattered agricultural communities.

Many families from the south of Scotland moved first to Ulster and then to America to escape poverty and make a new start. With them came a small number of Huguenots, like the Ashburn-Herndon family of the title story. Most of those associated families entered the country through Virginia into Pennsylvania. Soon they began to move southwestward in a continuing procession into the Carolinas, Tennessee, Georgia, and beyond, always searching for open space where they could pursue their independent ways. On the frontier everyone could start as equals. That was important to them.

THE HIGHLANDERS' DRAMATIC HISTORY sent them along a different path to the New World. From 1700 through the Highland clearances in 1800, Highlanders left Scotland in waves. Each surge of migration followed one of the savage tactics intended to make the Highland glens available for pasturing sheep. The first of the atrocities was the massacre at Glencoe in 1692. In the 1730s many left to escape overpopulation and poverty. Landlords drove Highlanders from their lands and burned their homes. In order to weaken the clans, a Hanoverian decree reduced the power of the chieftains and banned tartans, bagpipes, and weapons. The Highlanders' culture was basically demolished, and their numbers depleted. Their last desperate effort to keep their homes and way of life was the Second Jacobite Rebellion of 1745–46. When it collapsed with the defeat at Culladen, the remaining Highlanders fled Scotland in great numbers. The clearances of the early 1800s left only a sparse population in the glens. Many of that group entered America through the port of Charleston and settled in the mountains of western North Carolina. Ulster Scots of lowland origin and Highlanders merged in that relatively isolated mountain area where they kept their Scottish lifestyles. Some even continued to use the Scots-Gaelic language for years. Samuel Pinckney Taylor of "Sam and the Apples" left that Scottish environment to find cheap Texas ranchland. Other members of his family later followed. The Woods family and the related families you will meet in "The Sound of Clocks," "Seeing Ghosts," and "The Wagon Trail" were among the Ulster Scots in the westward movement into Texas. Both family groups brought along remnants of the old language, as in "The Song" and the Woods family's celebratory *ceilidhs*.

In this collection the names of some people and places have been changed for reasons of privacy. Others, like the Scottish name of Frances Monteith, the wife of the "fugitive doctor," have been left unaltered. Although her maiden name may sound foreign to a Texan's ear, residents of Scotland will recognize it as a variation of the Scots-Gaelic Menteith, a name known to them for centuries. Frances and her husband founded a large West Texas ranching family. Even now on Windham ranchlands, visitors receive typical Scottish hospitality that began with Frances. That hospitality is part of a quiet, almost secretive generosity that expects no notice or reward. You will see those traits in "The Boy," "The Stonemason," and "Different Grandmothers." In *The Line from Here to There*, Americans will find background information helpful in recognizing aspects of Scottish culture beyond the stereotypical images of tartans and bagpipes. I want them to know more about early Scottish American culture and the characteristics families have handed down unobtrusively through the generations from there to here.

At the time of the migrations, southern Scotland was largely rural. The small farmers had an enormous capacity for hard work and thrift to help them succeed. They believed the only measure of a man's worth was his own work. They had a great zeal to excel, but their accomplishment was not intended to elevate them to an upper class. In part, those who left Scotland were rebelling against a class system in which the "upper class" was destined from birth to become the only clerics and rulers. They abhorred the idle rich and were determined that all leaders, like the clan chieftains, should be chosen by peers for their proven abilities. To those leaders they willingly gave great loyalty.

The Scots have never been a submissive people, and historically they had not suffered imposed rule meekly. After a long series of wars, they were proud of their reputation as fierce warriors. In rural Scotland there was no organized law enforcement. The rule of law was that each individual was expected to right wrongs and defend himself against any injustice. In translation, Scotland's motto still reads, "No one attacks me with impunity." It is small wonder that the Scottish immigrants arriving in early Texas understood and accepted the law of the west. No doubt they helped to create that tradition.

One aspect of these new Americans' belief in equality and independence from imposed leaders made them strong advocates for education. They were determined that every man would be able to read and interpret the Bible for himself. He should not rely on a priestly hierarchy to interpret it for him. They fostered an equal but practical education with little attention to the arts or leisure activities. (Nollie's mother, Victoria Bell Ashburn, insisted on a school anywhere they settled.)

Scotland has produced many notable inventors, several of whom were notable even before 1800. Since that country was largely agricultural, it is not surprising that Cyrus Hall McCormick, a proud Scottish American, focused his inventive genius on farm implements. His inventions began a firm of international stature (see "A Company Christmas"). In the Scottish communities of North Carolina some of our families followed occupations they knew, like agriculture. They established small family farms with crops and livestock to meet their own needs. Some planted orchards. A few boat builders among our Barnett-Hamilton-Taylor family began to construct furniture. The stonecutters opened quarries. Years later, when the young state of Texas was ready to build a capitol, they brought Scottish stonecutters and masons to cut the pink granite and build the largest state capitol anywhere. When it was completed in 1888, they stayed. Later they constructed courthouses and buildings like Old Main on the campus of Southwestern University in Georgetown. Texans still cherish these architectural treasures.

When I was young I did not know much history of the Scottish people or how it had influenced me. I thought a West Texas upbringing had produced many of my traits and attitudes. Now I know some of those have been passed along for centuries. Although they have been modified along our line from there to here, they continue in the present generation. Remnants of old Scottish thinking have influenced some of our major life decisions, often without our awareness.

As a university professor of communication, I had always been interested in social and cultural influences on interpersonal communication. I had studied and developed literature for oral performance by groups and individuals. I had also researched and composed speeches for politicians and other public figures. But the family tales redirected my research interests. I began to study how such stories contributed to the listeners' concepts of self and family. Family stories speak volumes about the communication patterns in the family unit. They remind us who we are and who we wish to become.

Some of these stories are tales of my own ancestors or of extended family and friends. They tell of life experiences that measured character and produced a certain toughness of spirit that I associate with West Texans of Scottish heritage. Other stories are personal narratives of our more recent generations. These, too, are regional, reflecting a culture peculiar to the southwestern United States and specifically to the land of my roots—West Texas.

It is my hope that these stories of my family will inspire you to collect stories of your own, so that the people and places of your ancestry, too, may be remembered and celebrated for generations to come.

Texas Tartans

Long before I was old enough to go to school, I had learned almost everything that was important. Of course, like any child with older brothers and sisters, I was often told, "Oh, you don't know anything." But I knew a lot. For example, I knew about funerals and cemeteries. I went wherever the grown-ups went, so I had been to many funerals for relatives and family friends, for both the very old and very young. I was also a veteran of burials in city cemeteries, country churchyards, and private family plots on ranches. But the cemetery I knew best was Oak Grove Cemetery near where my parents grew up.

I had been there many times for services and with my grandmothers to tend the family plots. (There weren't perpetual-care cemeteries until I was almost grown.) I loved that cemetery with its huge oak and cedar trees and its tall ancient stones. I could find my way from the row of lots belonging to my father's family where my Grandmother Taylor had planted rosebushes, to the imposing Dodge family marker that marked the edge of the oldest section. From there I knew the way through a somewhat newer part to the plots belonging to my mother's family. You see, my maternal grandparents were newcomers. They hadn't arrived there until 1900. And you couldn't miss our Woods family plots because that grandmother always had rows of flowers blooming: daffodils and tulips in spring, zinnias and daisies in summer, pansies in fall and winter.

The part of that cemetery I loved most was the very oldest part where the stones were very tall and deeply carved. I learned to read many proper names from those stones that marked our associated families' plots: Murray, Livingstone, Wallace, and Hamilton, and others like McCullough, Graham, and Parsons. I spent a lot of time making up stories about those long-dead people and wondering why some died so young and what their relationship was to others on the same plot.

You see, I really did know a lot. For instance, I knew that old markers shaped like tree trunks were for the Woodmen of the World members. The ones with little carved lambs made me feel sad—they were for small children or babies. I knew that any stone showing a single finger pointing upward was probably for a Methodist, and that stones depicting the pearly gates open wide were nearly always for Baptists.

I hardly noticed those fancy crosses with circles at the center. I don't know why no one explained them to me. Maybe others in the family just accepted them unquestioningly, as I did, without knowing. I knew little family history, and I had never heard of the ancient Picts or Celts. I didn't even know what to call the Celtic crosses I saw there, where my Scottish grandmothers picked their way among the graves tending the flowers.

Now, I loved almost everything about visiting my parents' hometown because my father's brothers and sisters were usually there. They were a rowdy bunch, I guess, always joking, staying up half the night to play dominoes or 42, and playing pranks on each other. In that family no one was safe from the teasing, not even Grandmother Taylor. One morning while she was serving her usual hearty breakfast that always included huge bowls of oatmeal (*porridge* to Grandmother), one of them put sugar in her bowl when she wasn't looking. Now, Grandmother was adamant that porridge should be eaten with salt. When she tasted it, she sputtered and scowled. Then, still frowning, she got up and carried the dish outside for the cats. When she came back in she was laughing because she realized her children had tricked her. The sheer joy of being together seemed to make that family playful. Even when they gathered for funerals, they told stories, using humor to cope with their grief. That's how they taught me the purpose of a wake, and when they got together to do some chore for Grandmother, they made great fun of the whole job.

While that family was always playing games and joking, my mother's family introduced me to music. In that very musical group, everyone played two or three instruments. Sometimes Grandpapa's brothers came to visit and brought with them a wide variety of stringed instruments and a small hand drum. In the evenings they formed a family band and played together. Having a regular ceilidh, they called it. When they played tunes with "rhythm and snap," my aunts taught me Highland dances, and even steps like the Foursome Reel. By the time I was five or six, I could recognize an array of musical instruments by their sounds: fiddles and banjos, guitars and dulcimers, ocarinas, the mouth harp that my grandmother called the trump, several brass horns, and "the box"—the old-timers' name for the accordion. I had seen a picture of a man in kilts standing on a windy hillside playing the bagpipes. It was hanging on the wall in Grandpapa's office, but no one I knew played bagpipes. I didn't know a thing about bagpipes. I just loved the foot-tapping sound of the music when there was a family ceilidh.

Visits to my grandparents offered plenty of entertainment, but in the middle of it all my father always found time to slip away and drive across town to visit his elderly uncle and aunt. Sometimes I went, too, because I knew he liked to take me along. But I never felt very comfortable inside my great uncle's house. I didn't mind going in warm weather because we visited with them on their front porch, where there was an assortment of cats and dogs for me to pet. But in cold weather we went indoors. When I looked around that house, I understood why my grandmother said her sister-in-law "wasn't much for housekeeping."

The house had a dusty odor, and every furniture surface seemed to be cluttered with knickknacks. I had to sit quietly on the sofa among a collection of puffy pillows and a wool coverlet while the grown-ups talked. Everything around me looked like it had come together purely by chance. One pillow had orange hand-painted palm trees and the words *Souvenir of San Diego* across the front. Another was covered with bright pink and green crochet. And there was always a drab wool cloth thrown over the arm of the sofa. Like most children, I liked bright colors. I wondered if this dull piece of fabric had been brightly colored when it was new and had faded to a dull gray and tan with age. I thought it looked as old as Aunt Janie. It even *smelled* old. I thought it probably needed cleaning. My great uncle was quite a talker, so I had time to look at the pattern of that fabric until I knew every stripe and block of it. I could have recognized it anywhere. I ran my finger around the gray squares and traced the cross stripes of dull blue and brown. When my great aunt said she just loved to nap there, covered in "the plaid," I thought she was a little strange. I knew *I* didn't want to curl up under it, but somehow it did seem appropriate for Aunt Janie. Her gray hair almost matched some of the blocks in the cloth.

By age six I thought I knew quite a lot. Then I started to school, and in case I had missed the message from my older siblings, the first grade teacher made it clear: there was still a lot for me to learn. And I didn't even know that I didn't *know* about things like Celtic crosses, tartans, and bagpipes.

One day I came home from the first grade and said, "Daddy, what *are* we?"

He chuckled. "What do you mean?"

"Well, my friend Angelica and her brother were born in Mexico, and Betty in our class said her parents came from Greece, and at home they speak Greek. What are *we?*"

"Oh," he said, "We're all just Americans here."

"Well, when I told Gary and Herby that I thought *Mutschler* was a funny name, they said it was a German name. What's *Taylor?*"

"Oh," he began, "a long time ago people just had given names, like John or Robert. Then, to tell them apart, they would add something about the person, like the place where they lived. So John of Ross gradually was called John Ross, and John who was Robert's son became John Robertson. And some people were identified by their occupations, like John the Miller, or the Skinner, or the Tailor. Probably our name was an occupational name."

With all that new information to ponder, I didn't even realize he had avoided my question entirely. I guess he knew that sooner or later some relative would let me know "what we were." I was surprised, however, that spring when we went to my parents' hometown for Easter.

We arrived at my grandmother's house, and there were hugs all around. Then my grandmother looked me over, and as though she were flipping away a bug, she thumped the lapel of my coat and asked, "What's *that?*" Pleased to be noticed, I babbled importantly, "Oh, Grandmother, that's a shamrock. My teacher gave everybody one, and we had a Saint Patrick's Day party. We decorated the room, and everyone wore green. She said on Saint Patrick's Day everybody's Irish, and that from the looks of me, I obviously was!" I announced it all with the assurance of one who has just discovered her true identity.

"Well, you're *not,*" she said in a soft voice, but it sounded to me like she disapproved. I looked up at my dad. He grinned and winked at me, but when I took off my coat, I removed the little silk shamrock and tucked it way down in the bottom of my coat pocket. Now I figured that all I knew was what I *wasn't.* Not Greek, Mexican, or German. And now, I thought, even the teacher was wrong, and I wasn't Irish after all. But I still didn't know what I was.

That summer we went back to my parents' hometown for the funeral of a distant relative I had never known. In the procession we were riding in my uncle's Chevrolet, several cars back from the hearse. My uncle Roy was driving with my grandmother beside him in the front seat. She was wearing her best black dress with the white collar and cuffs. My aunt, my mother, and I occupied the back seat. The Texas summer heat was oppressive even with the car windows open, and my grandmother kept fanning steadily with a palm leaf fan.

Just inside the cemetery gate the whole procession came to a halt. We sat. When the car stopped, so did the breeze. I squirmed, and someone asked, "What are we waiting for?"

Grandmother kept fanning and looking straight ahead. She said quietly, "We'll wait for the pipes." That didn't make any sense, I thought. What did she mean? *What pipes?* I just wanted to be someplace cooler. I leaned toward the window on my right, trying to catch a bit of breeze. Two cemetery workmen near the car had stopped edging along the drive and had stepped back under a shade tree. Out of respect they removed their hats and stood, waiting for the procession to pass.

Just then, from across the cemetery, came a strange musical wail. I had never heard anything like it. My grandmother stopped fanning and sat up very straight and tall. One of the workmen outside my window said, "What's that commotion?" The older one said, "Oh, they're just burying one of those old red-headed Scots today."

The procession began to move again. I knew the way: two left turns back into the old section near the street. As we crept along I tried to see the source of that wailing, but the trees blocked my view until finally the procession halted near the family plots.

As we got out, I could see my father up ahead. He was helping a very old woman out of the first car. The strange music continued, and now I could see the piper way over near the wall. I stared in fascination. He looked like the picture on Grandpapa Woods's office wall. But there was no lonely hillside here. This piper was standing right there in the hot cemetery behind the long row of rose bushes I had watched my grandmother tend. He was *real*, and I fell in love with the forlorn tune he was playing.

The pallbearers started toward the open grave with the casket. That's when I saw it! That casket was draped with a familiar patterned fabric, the same dingy cloth my great aunt called "the plaid." I was astonished. I imagined someone actually removing that drab cloth—probably faded and maybe even a little dirty—from Great Aunt Janie's sofa and throwing it over the coffin. I still wonder.

It all seemed very odd to me and rather embarrassing. Didn't they know to put *flowers* on top of a casket? I hardly remember walking forward to join my father, but I pulled at his coat sleeve. "Why are we doing this?" I whispered. First the bagpipes, and now that plaid cloth.

He said softly, "We're just honoring an old man's wishes."

Well, now I know that dull-colored plaid has a name—the Muted Douglas—and I think it was probably used on the casket because there wasn't a piece of the Dress Douglas to be found in that little town, or anywhere else out in West Texas. I know several other tartans now, like the Hamilton and the Cameron. But I had just begun to learn about Celtic crosses, bagpipes, and tartans, and a lot of other cultural tidbits, such as why my grandmother called oatmeal *porridge* and thought it should be eaten with salt. I was just beginning to understand my very Scottish ancestry.

It wasn't until much later, however, that I understood what my father wanted me to know when I was making new friends in the first grade: that what matters most of all is that "we're all just Americans here."

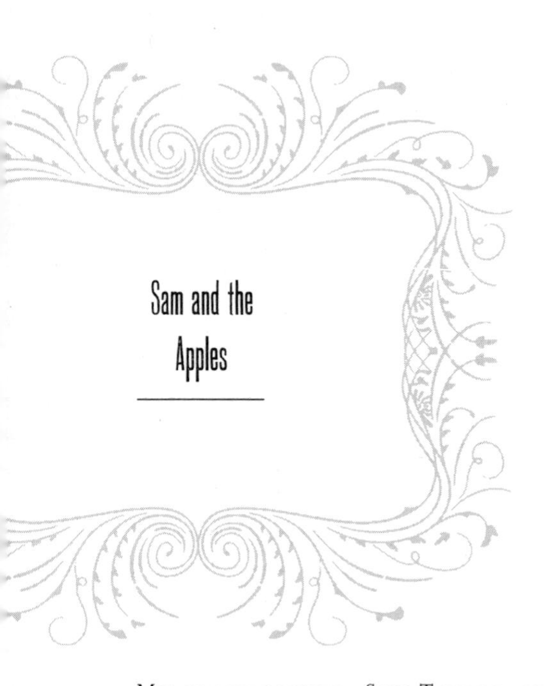

Sam and the Apples

My grandfather, Sam Taylor, was born in the mountains of western North Carolina in what was then, and still is, one of the nation's major apple-producing areas. Sam loved apples. As a boy, one of his favorite places in the whole world was his father's apple orchard. He spent many happy hours there, galloping in and out among the trees, mounted on his fine, imaginary horse, herding cattle along some western trail. Sometimes he chased down wayward yearlings, swinging an imaginary loop in the air above his head. He rested, sitting under a tree eating a crisp apple, and dreamed a small boy's dream of going out west to be a cowboy. But his father had other plans for Sam.

Sam stayed in school, and in time he became a professor of mathematics. The young ladies in the school admired the tall, auburn-haired bachelor, and he returned their smiles, but his head was filled with another dream. Often when his students were working at their problems, Sam gazed out the window at the blue-green of the Great Smoky Mountains and dreamed a young man's dream of going west to be a rancher. Because he didn't marry, he was able to save his money, and by the time he was in his mid-thirties, he thought he had saved enough to buy some cheap Texas ranchland.

The year the railroad came through the mountains, Sam loaded his horse and his favorite dog onto a railway car and went down the mountain, heading west to be a rancher. The whole family gathered at the railway station to see him off. His mother handed him a big lumpy bag, saying, "These are apples for your trip, but son, they tell me there are no trees in Texas. I don't know how you can live in a place where they can't grow apples." Later that night she opened the family Bible, and by the lamp's glow she looked at Sam's name and date of birth. To the right, she carefully wrote three letters, *G.T.T.*, and the date. Little did she know that she would write those letters in the Bible time after time as her younger sons followed Sam westward. Seen in many Southern family Bibles, the inscription was considered to be as final as death. *G.T.T.* meant *Gone To Texas*.

When Sam arrived in North Texas, he began to look for suitable land to buy. Then one evening when he returned to his lodgings, there were two well-dressed men waiting for him. They said, "Mr. Taylor, could we speak with you? We understand that you are a mathematics professor. We represent Westminster Baptist Academy, and we are in need of someone with your credentials to teach mathematics." Sam took the position, and in his free time he made long rides to inspect available ranchland. On those solitary trips he pondered the difference and the distance of this empty western land from the Carolina mountains of home.

Then Sam met a young woman named Christianna Elizabeth Bradley. She was only half his age, but her shy ways, long red hair, and grass green eyes haunted him. She soon became a part of his dream of life on the range. To his surprise, Sam had fallen in love. He called her "Miss Annie." She blushed and giggled when people teased them about "all those red-headed young'uns" the two red-haired parents were sure to have. Together they moved farther west to ranch.

Ranchers on neighboring lands wondered whether this professor from the East was tough enough to raise cattle. He was. Sam and Christianna learned to improve their breeding stock, encourage the best grasses, and conserve water. As their herd of livestock grew, so did their brood of red-haired children. Sam began to expand their land holdings. When people took note, he joked, "I'm not really a greedy man—I just sort of like the idea of owning all the land that joins mine."

Since he prided himself on being progressive, Sam was one of the first in the county to own an automobile. He became a familiar sight driving along the road between the ranch and the town. Occasionally he honked the bulb horn to tell people that Sam Taylor was coming, and they should get their horses under control so they wouldn't bolt at the sight of his car.

Driving along that road, he often lamented that apple trees did not thrive on dry West Texas ranchland. He thought of his friend, Josh Rickman, whose father had come to that county a generation earlier, homesteaded land along a creek, and planted apple trees. Although Sam was proud of his own ranch, he envied Josh that apple orchard. He knew Josh would never sell the orchard to him, but Sam dearly loved apples. The older he grew, the more he thought about the apple orchards of his childhood.

As Sam aged, his eyesight began to fail. One day, two of his sons insisted, "Dad, you have to stop driving that automobile. It's dangerous for you to be out on the road in that contraption." He stopped driving the car, but it didn't slow him down much. He just dusted off the buggy that was still in his barn and hitched up a horse named Sunny. After all, he mused, he had owned Sunny longer than the automobile. Sunny knew every nearby road, took him where he wanted to go, and never ended up in a ditch.

One morning, Sam hitched Sunny to the buggy for a trip to town. He had one stop to make at a neighboring ranch, and then he planned to meet one of his sons at the cattle auction. As he went down the lane toward the gate, he squinted his eyes to see Miss Annie in her garden. She was pulling onions, shaking off the sand, and placing them on a small cart. Sam smiled and waved to her. She was still so energetic she never seemed to tire of gardening. Best of all, he thought, she never seemed to get tired of an old man like him.

When he was out on the road, he turned toward the next ranch, where he was going to talk to his neighbor Robert Wallace about some heifers. He strained his weak eyes to look over his pastures, and as he neared the Wallaces' gate, he could see a wagon and team approaching in the distance. Even with his dim sight, he recognized the team, and then the driver. It was his friend, Josh Rickman. Sam pulled Sunny over near the gate and waited. As Josh stopped, Sam could see that the wagon was piled high with a load that glistened red in the morning sun. His mouth watered.

He called out, "Mornin', Josh. Mighty fine load you have there."

"Sure is, Sam," Josh grinned. "Good crop this year. More than I can use. I hope to sell this load in town."

"Well," Sam sighed, "As you pass my place, just turn in and leave about a hundred pounds of them with Miss Annie. She'll know what to do with them."

"I'll sure do it, Sam." Josh nodded, touched the brim of his hat, spoke to his team, and was gone. He didn't even ask why Sam needed so many. There was no mention of price or payment. After all, the old friends had been doing business with a nod of the head or a handshake for more than thirty years.

Sam took care of his business at the Wallace place and then headed into town where he met his son John at the auction barn. By late afternoon he was on the road home. Along the way he squinted at the pastures of late-summer dry grass and thought again of the blue-green of the Great Smoky Mountains where he had spent his Carolina childhood. It had been a long day, and Sam was tired. With the warm sun on his back and the steady *clop, clop, clop* of Sunny's hooves on the hard-packed road, the reins began to go slack in his hands. He dozed and dreamed an old man's dream, that he was a boy again among the trees of his father's apple orchard.

As they neared the ranch gate, Sunny's gait quickened, waking Sam from his dream with a start. Even his old eyes could see that the land around him was not an orchard, but his own yellow-brown pasture. He thought, "Well, at least tonight I'll have a crisp apple or two. If Miss Annie left the garden in time to bake, perhaps there'll even be a hot apple pie."

On the lane he could see the blurry outline of the house in the distance, and soon he thought he saw a figure standing on the porch. As the image cleared, he could see the shape of the fiery Miss Annie. She was standing with feet apart and hands on her hips. Every inch of her stance signaled trouble. He sighed and thought, "There are some disadvantages in having married a much younger woman." He reined up near the porch, greeting her with, "Evenin', Miss Annie. What seems to be the problem?" She didn't even wait for Sunny to come to a complete stop.

She shouted back, "Sam Taylor, have you lost your *mind?!*"

He replied with his usual calm, "Well, if I have, I haven't missed it yet."

She didn't even pause. "Sam, I have a world of onions. I've been pulling onions all day. I've hung the rafters in the barn full of onions. I have a cellar full of onions." She waved her hand toward the garden, "There are two rows of onions out there I haven't even pulled yet. So, what in thunder do you think I'm going to do with a hundred pounds of Josh Rickman's *big red onions?!*"

The Line from Here to There

In the 1870s a traveler finding his way west from Fort Worth followed a thin brown line, a barely visible wagon trail, that stretched out in a great curve across West Texas. It was the route of the old Butterfield-Overland Stagecoach Line. And in the late 1870s this was the route taken by George Kempton Ashburn. He left his wife and three small girls in the relative safety of Fort Worth and went west on horseback in search of land to homestead. But before he left, his wife, Victoria, made him promise that he wouldn't take them anyplace far away from a church and a school.

The first few days west of Fort Worth, George still saw houses with neatly fenced yards and a scattering of live oaks among the gently rolling hills. It looked a little like home, but as he kept west, the hills gave way to a slow, steady rise in the land, and only an occasional house or chimney could be seen.

By the fourth day, the land rose before him with increasing barrenness, and the live oaks grew sparse. Houses, fences, and all signs of settlers were disappearing. After the first long climb through the *cheniere* (locally called "shinnery"), which scraped against him as he rode, even the scrub oak vanished.

One night George camped at the abandoned Fort Phantom Hill, near where the Butterfield trail began curving south. Where the brown line wound southward, he left the trail and rode northwest. He kept remembering stories told by his brother J.B., who had gone west to hunt buffalo. Plentiful game, and vast open spaces. Those stories stirred a boyhood dream of exploring unknown lands.

He climbed the Caprock until he found a place he'd heard about but only half believed. There before him was a land that stretched from horizon to horizon as level as his mother's dining table. Over it all was an enormous canopy of bright blue sky.

No trail, no path, no houses or fences, no trees. He squinted. From where he stood to the very edge of the world, it seemed was nothing but tall, shimmering grass. George loved its endlessness. He felt a kind of freedom he had never known before.

Now, George was a conservative sort, a shopkeeper who always sang hymns softly in church lest someone nearby hear him hit a note off key. But here he felt compelled to sing. Loudly. For days he rode, singing with great abandon, belting out stanza after stanza of all the songs he knew. He even sang "Old One Hundred" at the top of his lungs.

Gradually, as he became accustomed to the wide expanse of prairie grass, he began wondering what his wife Victoria would think about it. Victoria Bell was better educated than most women, but it was an education that equipped her best to be a gracious southern lady. So after weeks of carefree exploration, George doubled back somewhat to the south and east and finally found a place that almost met Victoria's requirements. Almost.

In a tiny community called Fairview stood three or four houses, two half dugouts, and the rough framework of a tiny church. He liked the people, and the land was fertile. The church building was nearly complete, and over the weeks George lent a hand with the final construction. By the time the church was finished George had convinced those people that they should have a school as well. Six and a half miles away, he picked a site for a house.

Now, in a land with no trees, most houses were built of stone, sod, or picket. George sent to Fort Worth for lumber, built himself a dugout against a low slope, and started the stone foundations for a house and barn. He cleared a garden plot. That first long winter he lived in the half dugout. He worked early and late, whenever the weather permitted. Ice storms forced him to stop for days at a time. George would lie in the dugout and listen to the wind, praying that the cold would break early, so the mule teams could get through with their wagons of lumber.

When spring came, George planted the garden. His neighbors came to help him raise the house and barn. Then he rode back to Fort Worth for Victoria and their three little girls. The oldest was nine. Her name was Alice Juanita Norroway Ashburn, but that was such a long name for such a little girl that they always called her "Nollie." The next was Lillie, the seven-year-old tomboy. And then there was tiny Annie who turned six somewhere along the trail west of Fort Worth.

Now, the journey by covered wagon was long, and the girls pestered their father with questions about the other children in the community, about the teacher and the school, and about how they would make their way to school. "How far is it? And how will we get there?" George said he would build a two-wheeled wooden cart just big enough for three girls. He would buy a horse, and they could go to school by horse and cart. Because Nollie was the oldest, she would drive them to school. The younger girls bounced excitedly at the prospect, but Nollie looked out at the empty space that looked the same in all directions, and she worried, "How will we find our way?" There were no fence lines to follow. She didn't see *anything* she could use as a landmark. Well, with great humor, George dismissed her worries. With a broad wave of his arm, he said, "Don't you worry about it, Nollie! I'll just draw a line from the house to the school." She asked, "But how will I find my way?" And again her father said, "Don't worry, dear. I really will draw a line from here to there." Then he laughed. But Nollie didn't find it funny, and she worried.

When the group arrived at the community of Fairview, they loved the new house, and for a time Nollie set aside her fears about getting to school. In the evenings and on rainy days, George worked away in the shed, building the cart. He taught Nollie to hitch Clancy, an older, gentle horse, to the cart and showed her how to handle the reins. She practiced making the turns around the house, past the garden, around the barn, and back again, until she felt quite confident. On Sundays George loaded his family into the buckboard and took them to church across the open prairie where there was no road, no trail, not even the suggestion of a path. The scenery looked exactly the same in all directions, and Nollie strained to see a boulder or tree for a landmark. When she didn't find one, she worried. Silently she considered that in the morning the sun would be on her left, and in the evening the sun would again be on her left. That was all the assurance she had of the way to go. As they rode along, the girls played a game to see who could catch the first glimpse of the church in the distance.

Then one morning in late summer, as Victoria stood ironing the dress that Annie would wear for her first day of school, the girls looked out to see their father plowing. But he wasn't plowing the garden. In fact, he seemed to have started at the barn. He walked along behind the mule, huffing and plowing a single furrow off in a strange direction. And Lillie, the tomboy, ran after him shouting, "Papa, what are you doing plowing over *there?* Papa! I don't think that's even our land!" George stopped and wiped his face on his sleeve. He waved. "It's all right, Lillie. I'll be back by dinner time." Then he called to the mule and forced the plow into the hard ground again.

All day long the girls wondered where their father was going and why he was plowing away into the distance. Their mother only smiled. But late in the afternoon they looked up to see him coming back along the same furrow. He was plowing the same line, making it wider and deeper.

As he washed up for dinner he said, "Nollie, you don't need to worry anymore, my dear. I've drawn a line from here to there." And George Kempton Ashburn had plowed a single furrow *six and a half miles long,* across virgin grassland from the house to the schoolyard, to guide his little girls across the open range to school.

The following Sunday George said, "Girls, today you're going to lead the way in your cart, and your mother and I will follow in the buckboard." And as Nollie drove along, she could see, stretching far into the distance through the tall grass, a thin brown line leading her straight to school.

Well, by the time the girls were grown that single furrow had become a path, and then a trail, and finally a road. But in the beginning, it was only a narrow brown line.

The little cart their father built had a single board bench that lifted up on leather hinges to reveal a compartment under the seat. That's where the girls could put their lunches and books, and the oilcloth rain capes their mother made for them, because the little cart had no top. When it rained, they had to be prepared to put on the capes and stay as dry as they could.

Now, riding to school by horse and cart was a lot of fun at first, but soon after school began the weather turned cold. Six and a half miles in an open cart is a long way when the sharp winter wind blows down from the Texas Panhandle. And when the sleet and snow began, their mother took thin, flat rocks and put them into the fireplace until they were very hot. Then she would slide them out on boards and set them on the floor of the little cart. The girls put their feet on the heated rocks so they stayed toasty warm all the way to school. But as the cart bounced through the wind, their noses and fingers soon ached with cold, even inside their mittens and scarves.

Finally the weather warmed. Early spring brought drenching rains. And though it was warmer, six and a half miles in an open cart in a cold spring rain is not a lot of fun.

One afternoon after school, as the three prepared for their trip home, the teacher said, "Girls, you'd better hurry along. There's a storm coming." In the distance to the north they could see a wall of black clouds. Lightning flickered, and as they started out, the low rumble of thunder made Nollie hurry the horse as fast as she could along the thin brown line. Gradually, it began to rain hard. The lightning grew close and the thunder got louder, and Annie began to cry.

Then all at once right in front of them there came an enormous stroke of lightning and a deafening clap that frightened the little horse. He reared and bolted crazily away from the brown line. The bit in his teeth, he jerked the cart behind him into the high grass. Nollie tried to control him, but she lost her grip on the reins.

Soon one wheel of the cart hit a rock. And it bounced little Annie right out onto the muddy ground. Clancy just kept running, his eyes wild. The cart pitched in a zigzag path through the grass. Nollie and Lillie were now sprawled on the floor of the cart, clinging for dear life and screaming at Clancy to stop. But he didn't stop. He ran and ran and ran, until he was tired.

As the horse slowed, Nollie recovered the reins. Trembling, the girls brushed themselves off and stood up to get a look at where they were. But as far as they could see, there was nothing but grass. They called and called for Annie, but she didn't answer. Dark clouds covered the afternoon sun, and they couldn't see a brown line *anywhere.*

But Nollie had presence of mind. She said, "Lillie, you stand right here. I'll drive the horse in a circle, and we'll find where our wheels made ruts in the mud. Where the wet grass is knocked down, we'll see how we came. If we follow that route, we'll find Annie, and then we can find our way home." Nollie tried to sound confident, but Annie was only six, and it was getting dark. Nollie knew about mountain lions and lobo wolves.

So Nollie guided the horse and cart in a careful circle until she found the ruts their wheels had cut as they came through the high, wet grass. Then they picked their way along the wild path the horse had made across the prairie. From time to time they stopped to look for Annie, and Lillie would even stand up on the bench and call, "Annie! . . . Annie!" But there was no answer. They rode farther, now and then calling "Annie!" Finally, from way in the distance, they heard a tiny voice pleading, "Nollie, come and get me. I'm cold." And they knew they had found her.

Well, they brushed off some of the mud, picked out the grass burrs, gave her a big hug, and put her in the cart between them. Then they began to look for the thin brown line. They hadn't gone far from the furrow when Annie had been thrown out of the cart, so it didn't take long for them to locate it and follow the furrow home.

By the time they neared the house it was nearly pitch dark. They could see their mother standing in the driving rain, anxiously scanning the brown line. Victoria Ashburn was within days of delivering her fourth child. She was relieved to see her girls.

NOW, I CAN TELL YOU that those three little girls had long, eventful lives. Nollie lived to be almost ninety-one. She became my husband's Grandmother Herndon, who raised him after his mother's death. She never tired of telling about the day when the horse ran away with the cart and dumped Annie in the stickers and mud, or about the thin brown line their father plowed from here to there to show them the way to school.

The Fugitive Doctor

PEOPLE HAVE COME TO EXPECT TO HEAR ME TELL STORIES from my own family. This story, though, was told to me by my friend Paula Windham. It's about her ancestor, John Darby Windham, a pioneer doctor born in Mississippi Territory in the early 1800s, who became the patriarch of a large Texas ranching family. As I tried to piece together the details of the doctor's history, I learned that each one of the Windhams had a different take on what John Darby Windham had done and where he had done it. We do know that he was well known for his hospitality to strangers and that he was a man of no great physical stature—barely five feet one. But in time he cast a long shadow across Texas.

Paula Windham is his great-granddaughter. Since her retirement from the university, she lives on the ranch that has been home to her for most of her life. Paula has more houseguests than anyone I've ever known. Despite the fact that the Sand Hills Ranch is almost an hour from the nearest real city, there is a steady procession of visitors. They all know Paula will welcome them even when they arrive unannounced and stay for days. You should see the crowd on Christmas Eve. Sometimes there are seventy-five or eighty of us filling the brightly decorated rooms with food and conversation. Paula bustles through the crowd to see that all are greeted and fed. There's even a gift under the tree for every guest! It takes a week to put up all the lights and decorations to achieve the final effect. There's always someone's daughter-in-law from away, wearing velvet and a tiny diamond pendant, who stares speechless at the array of piñatas, serapes, and red chili pepper *ristras* hung from the rustic cedar posts.

A stream of cars and pickups travel the mile and a half from the ranch gate to the house, watching for cattle. It's often necessary to stop a time or two to urge livestock off the road. One year Paula was in the living room making large red bows to decorate the fence posts around the front yard when two or three fellows came in from working cattle all day. Button, a seasoned cowpoke, exclaimed, "Paula, you're just decoratin' the whole place! What're you gonna do with so many big red bows?" Paula couldn't resist. With a twinkle in her eye she said, "Oh, I thought it'd be cute if we tied 'em around the necks of the cows in that front pasture to greet people as they drive in for the party. Would you help me tie them on, on Christmas Eve day?" Button couldn't believe his ears, but he'd have done anything for Paula. He thought she was serious. Shifting his weight from one boot to the other, he envisioned the nightmare of trying to tie ribbons around the necks of a herd of unwilling, slobbery cows. He drawled, "Well, if that's what you want to do, I guess I could come help you." And Paula began to laugh.

Even with the bows on the fence posts instead of the cattle, the party is an impressive affair. A short hallway separates the two largest rooms in the ranch house, and I always pause there in front of a particular photograph. In it a diminutive elderly man with a white beard sits in a tall wicker chair. The top of his head rests far below the top of the chair back, and his wife sits by his side. The two of them appear unruffled and completely at ease with the mob of assorted family and friends milling through the house. Some people come in jeans, boots, and wide-brimmed hats, and the city folks wear their glittering holiday finery. There are children in Sunday school clothes, and some of us just looking well scrubbed but comfortable. I know that the man in the photograph was a pioneer and local legend. I always think he would be pleased to see his descendents welcoming everyone who comes to the door. In spite of the conflicting tales of his exploits, Dr. J. D. Windham was always known as a gracious host.

Dr. Windham became a widower as a young man. His wife died shortly after the birth of their first child, and soon the young doctor began making house calls with his tiny son in tow. In 1836 the new Republic of Texas began advertising across the South, promising opportunities for professional people, especially doctors. Dr. Windham took his little son west and settled in East Texas, where he set up a medical practice and became active in local politics. In those early days, the practice of medicine was a hybrid of folk remedies with a little science thrown in, and like many of the Native American healers, Dr. Windham was known to have been in possession of a *madstone*. Such a stone was taken from the gut of a deer or antelope. It was useful in addressing snakebite or the bite of a rabid animal. The healer held the stone to the bite and then, it was said, the stone "took hold of the wound" and drew the poison out of the afflicted person. The stone made Dr. Windham much sought-after, and people rode long distances to see him and receive this treatment.

In 1841 he married Frances Monteith, and in time the two had a large family. When the Civil War began, Dr. Windham's older sons and his brothers-in-law became soldiers, and the doctor stayed at home as part of the Home Guard. There were great political tensions in East Texas during that time, some of which turned violent, and that fact may account in part for the events that followed.

Now whether or not Dr. Windham was actually involved in a crime of any kind is not truly known, but in 1865 a grand jury did indict him on two counts of murder. In the flowery language of the period, two long documents allege in detail how the doctor took "a certain rope," placed it around the neck of John Gann, and hanged him, causing Mr. Gann to die instantly. The following page of the same indictment states that Dr. Windham took "a particular pistol," put it to the head of John Gann, and shot him just behind his left ear—a wound from which, the document states, for a second time, that Mr. Gann died instantly. The second indictment describes the murder of a William Burris in exactly the same manner, alleging that J. D. Windham both hanged and shot Mr. Burris, causing him to die instantly *twice*. What really happened? No one really knows.

Dr. Windham was never brought to trial for killing those two men four times because the whole Windham family quickly moved west to Brown County. There he established the county's first medical practice and, together with his sons, started a ranch on Lower Pecan Bayou. The doctor was known as a man of a generous and caring nature—a gracious host who welcomed every stranger and treated everyone the same way. Many stories tell of his long trips to treat patients without concern about being paid for his services. He was dearly loved and greatly admired, but after a few years the bounty hunters appeared.

A group of heavily armed men stopped in the town of Brownwood asking directions to the Windham place. One person after another referred them to a young physician who admired old Dr. Windham. The young man gave the riders a long and scenic set of directions to the Windham ranch, whereupon they set out. The young doctor then sent a lone rider across country by the quickest route to warn his friend.

On receiving news that the pursuers were on their way, Dr. Windham stationed his sons and sons-in-law out of sight in strategic positions and told them to wait. When the bounty hunters rode into the yard later that afternoon, the men of the family rose up everywhere—from behind trees, woodpiles, and outbuildings. Guns drawn, they surrounded the riders. At that point Dr. Windham made his appearance through the front door. He strode out onto the wide porch and with a warm smile said, "Good afternoon, gentlemen. I assume you've come for dinner."

What could the bounty hunters do? Disarmed, they dismounted and were wined and dined with the Windhams' usual hospitality. Two or three days later they rode away without the diminutive doctor.

In time other bounty hunters came, stopping along the way to recruit a posse. On ranch after ranch their prospects asked them, "Who are we goin' after?" When they heard the name of their friend, the only doctor for a hundred miles or so, they refused to ride.

The bounty hunters sought Dr. Windham repeatedly but never succeeded in raising a posse against him. Even the Texas Rangers gave it a try, until they were told, "Look, fellas, nobody around here will ever help you bring in John Windham. He's no outlaw, and besides, he's the only doctor we've got. If you do try to get him, everybody around here will be right there to make sure you don't!" One old man related how the doctor had fixed him up when a bull gored him and broke his ribs, and another told how Dr. Windham had cared for his wife and children for weeks when they took sick, never once concerned that the man couldn't pay him a dime. The stories went on and on, until the Rangers must have concluded they had worse criminals to pursue. At that point even the bounty hunters gave up and never came back.

In 1874 the Windhams and most of their grown children moved farther up Pecan Bayou into southern Callahan County to a place known as Tecumseh Peak. There Dr. Windham set up a medical practice, built a large general store with a pharmacy, and began to acquire ranchland. His sons ran the store, which became a regular stop along the trail for settlers traveling west, and they took care of the ranching business. In time a sizable community grew up around the Windham place. Dr. and Mrs. Windham even founded the first church in the area, the congregation meeting in their home until the final building was completed. It was a small empire of sorts, so much so that just about everything in those parts must have begun to feel as if it belonged to them.

Now, from time to time it was rumored that the Windham boys were a bit too enthusiastic about affixing their brand to stray livestock. They were a rowdy bunch, but the family was known for their generosity and hospitality to everyone who came their way. In that county and those surrounding, there was no other doctor, and Dr.

Windham's skill became legend across West Texas. The sick came long distances to consult him, and patients often stayed as guests in the second-story rooms of the doctor's own house, even for months of convalescence.

All the while, the Texas Rangers kept a handbook of fugitives. Some called it "The Book of Knaves," and others referred to it as "The Rangers' Bible." In it, one entry read, "John D. Windham, wanted on 2 counts of murder, 5'1" tall, blue eyes, gray hair, about 72 years old, very accomplished medical doctor. Last known to be living in Callahan County in the practice of medicine."

Dr. John Darby Windham, indicted but never tried, lived well into his eighties and died peacefully in his own bed. He is buried in Tecumseh Cemetery beside his wife, Frances. Nearby, successive generations of the Windham family are still ranching on Windham lands that stretch across Callahan County. Like the little doctor, they are known to be gracious hosts. They take great pride in their heritage and good-naturedly tolerate the teasing they sometimes hear about their ancestor, the fugitive doctor.

Several years ago, Paula Windham and I were gathering up old western items from her barn to use as decorations for a party. As I looked over bales of hay, old saddles and tack, and some cast iron pots, I came across a pile of rusty branding irons. I held one up and said, "Paula Windham, what are you doing with this running iron?" A running iron has only one purpose—to alter an existing cattle brand. Paula laughed and said, "Every ranch needs one!"

Safe from Wolves

Over the years the Hollywood film industry has given quite a lot of attention to the American West, but the result often makes the early history of the cattle country where I live seem a bit more glamorous than it really was.

I grew up listening to elderly people tell firsthand accounts of those early days in West Texas, and I can assure you that while those settlers were interesting people, their lives were anything but glamorous. Their first dwellings were often half dugouts built along an incline. Others lived in what we call "picket houses." Since there were too few big trees to build log homes, slim posts were set vertically to make the walls of a picket house. Later, permanent dwellings were built out of adobe or stone. Military forts, as well as houses, were constructed of stone.

Most homes had few windows because glass was scarce. Those who did put in window openings often covered them with hides or boarded them up for the winter. Sideboards from a wagon were even used sometimes to cover windows. When warm weather returned, the boards and hides came off, and windows were left open. Those early dwellings were crude protection from weather or any other threat.

One Thursday when I was about four years old, I went with my mother to an all-day quilting. I especially remember one white-haired woman who bent close to the fabric as she worked. Another youngster and I played near the quilt frame, a wooden rectangle that clamped the edges of the quilt to hold it taut. After a while the two of us crept into the open space underneath the quilt. We could still hear the grown-up conversation—sometimes low, steady, and indecipherable, and other times faster and louder—until at last the dark quilt shook with their laughter. Above our heads the talk at the quilting frame turned to the quilters' earliest memories.

At one end of the quilt the white-haired woman began to speak. At least a generation older than my mother, she had lived in one of those crude dwellings on the plains. There had been an earthen floor, and windows and a door left uncovered in summer.

Her family boasted no luxuries. A double washtub served for both laundry and bathing, but the only water came from a stream that flowed some distance from the house. Her mother carried water from that stream. But, the other women wanted to know, how did she protect her baby and toddler from wild animals and other dangers when she had to go for water?

The woman's voice rasped on. My little friend had crept off toward other interests, but I stayed quiet. The woman said that her earliest memory was of being left *under the washtub* with her baby sister. Her mother propped up one end of the tub with a flat rock to provide a couple of inches of space, for air. Then she placed large stones on top to keep animals from overturning the tub.

Mesmerized, I crouched in the dim light under the quilt frame.

"My job was to stay underneath and keep the baby quiet. When she cried, how the sound reverberated off the metal sides of that tub! Her screams were deafening, and I tried to cover her mouth with my hands. But even when the baby kept still, sometimes animals came . . . *wolves*," she said. "I could hear them. Sometimes I could even see their noses sniffing along the opening between the dirt floor and the washtub's edge."

"The time seemed eternal," she went on, "waiting in the dark for my mother to come back and scare them away."

That story was so vivid that it has stayed with me for a lifetime.

At night sometimes as a child I would huddle in the dark underneath the covers of my own warm, safe bed and try to imagine what it would have been like to live on the prairie long ago—to stay under a metal washtub where wolves sniffed only inches away.

As a young single mother working to provide for two small children while teaching and going to graduate school, I thought often of that pioneer mother, forced to protect her children in such a primitive way. That story of wolves and a washtub blends for me with other stories, many from my own family, to put my own life in proper perspective. I have never doubted that those early West Texans were strong people, and their strength reminds me of my own.

No wonder my generation, raised during the Great Depression and World War II, understood from older family members that we were supposed to be tough enough to cope with whatever came our way. We came from sturdy stock.

I have no idea who that small, white-haired woman was. I never heard my mother call her by name. But I hope that she told that story to her own family, so that later generations know what the early West was really like, and what strong pioneers they sprang from.

"Chocolate"

I AM A CHILD OF THE GREAT DEPRESSION. I GREW UP IN A small West Texas town where there was a large Hispanic population but very few African Americans. The few black people I knew were adults and, since it was the 1930s, I knew them only by their first names. Even a distinguished gray-haired gentleman who worked for a local department store I knew only as *James*.

Now, occasionally some black citizen in our town was given a title of respect, usually in deference to his or her great age. The title was *Aunt* or *Uncle*. That was the case with Aunt Georgia. She was a tiny, wrinkled woman who lived in a small apartment behind the big house next door to us.

Aunt Georgia had been born into slavery. She was "about eight years old," she guessed, at the time of the emancipation.

Next to her apartment there was a shed, and inside it sat several large trunks with padlocks on them. The older children in the neighborhood whispered to us that those trunks were full of money! But I know now that wasn't true, because Aunt Georgia was a retired schoolteacher. Any teacher can guess what she really kept in those trunks—books, letters from favorite students, and little mementos that dearly remembered children had made for her years ago. Aunt Georgia loved children. And she always had time for me.

Then there was Lillian. Lillian was a warm, smiling woman who supplied all the parenting and most of the love I knew for the first few years of my life, and because it was 1934 and I was four years old, I took for granted the fact that I called her "my Lillian" and *she* called *me* "Miss Rosy."

The world was still small to me then, a swirl of people, of comings and goings that revolved around the house on Third Street, the first place I remember as *home*.

Along behind the house was a wide graveled alleyway that ran for several blocks through the town. It came to a dead-end up the street to the west at the First Christian Church, which marked the official beginning of the business district. That alley was the scene of just about all the cultural activity I was aware of in my young life. It was a great place for the neighborhood children to play.

Now I was the only small child in the neighborhood except for my best friend, Peppy Herndon, or "Pep" for short. He lived across the street, and every afternoon he came walking past with his grandfather on the way to the next block to visit his great-grandmother, who was quite ill. Sometimes he got to stop and play. But, because we were only four, we were not allowed to cross the street alone, so most of the time I just tagged along behind the older children.

I was always at their heels on long summer evenings. That's when the adults sat on their front porches to watch the traffic pass, water their lawns, or just visit with neighbors, while the children played hide-and-seek along the alleyway. I wasn't very good at the game. I usually hid in the same place every time, or I giggled and got caught. Nevertheless, *my mother said* they had to let me play.

One day into that familiar scene came a boy like no other I had ever known. I'll never forget the first time I saw him. The older girls were making mud pies in the alley behind our house. They were taking the "dough" from my mother's flower bed, patting it out thin, and cutting it into shapes with old, rusty cookie cutters. Then they peeled the pieces out and set them on a row of bricks at the edge of the alleyway to dry. Pep and I were playing nearby. We looked up to see the older boys coming down the alley from the west, and with them was a child we had never seen before. He was a boy of perhaps six or seven, tall for his age and thin. He had enormous brown eyes and curly, curly hair, almost as red as mine.

As they came down the alley, one of the older boys scooped up one of the mud pies and, with a smirk, took the new boy firmly by the arm. He said, "Hey, you like *chocolate?* How about a piece of fudge?" He thrust one of the mud pies into the boy's hand. I saw him lift it slowly toward his face. I yelled, "Hey, don't! That's . . ." But about that time one of the older boys stepped in front of me, grabbed me by the shoulders, and said, "Shut up, runt! You'll ruin everything." By the time I had wiggled free and stepped out where I could see again, the boy was chewing solemnly. The bigger boy was saying, "Pretty good, isn't it? You like *fudge*, don't you?" The boy swallowed and nodded silently. "Here. Have another one, chocolate boy," demanded the older boy.

The name stuck. Everyone in the neighborhood called him "Chocolate." I never knew his real name, but Chocolate and I became great friends that summer. He had time to play with me when the older children didn't. He coached me at hide-and-seek. He was *good* at it! He knew all the best places to hide and showed me how to be very, very still. He said that if I could keep still long enough, I could become *invisible*.

During the daytime we played in the sand pile behind my house or on the swing. Sometimes we sat on a stone bench next to the fishpond and fed stale crackers to the fish. Sitting there, we listened to Aunt Georgia tell us tales about faraway places. She called it *geography*. I could tell Aunt Georgia enjoyed our company.

I did notice, however, that when Chocolate was there Lillian always seemed to be a little bit out of sorts. Oh, she brought milk and cookies to the stone bench in the backyard, but more than once I heard her say, "Your daddy's somebody special in this town. You ought not to be playing with the likes of *him." The likes of him?* I only knew that Chocolate was my friend.

Well, one late summer evening the older children were all gone somewhere except for one big boy named Zach. Zach and I tried to play hide-and-seek, but it's just not a lot of fun if there are only two. Zach finally had a great idea. We would go up the alley to see if Chocolate could come and play because Chocolate was so good at hide-and-seek. As we went up the alley, I stretched out my legs as far as I could, trying to match my steps to Zach's longer stride. I felt very proud to be going somewhere with an older boy who was not my brother.

As we came to the side street, I knew I was not supposed to cross, but I wasn't going to admit that to Zach. So I hesitated just a bit. Then we crossed the side street into the alley of the next block. There was a large, gray Packard parked in the alleyway. We circled the Packard and found ourselves at the base of a wooden stairwell leading up to a garage apartment. I knew where we were then. We were directly behind the Herndon house, the home of Pep's great-grandmother. Chocolate lived there with his mother, who took care of the elderly Mrs. Herndon.

When I looked way up I could see through the screen door into the kitchen at the top of the stairs. To the right of the door stood a woman cooking dinner. In the center of the room a single light bulb dangled from a cord. Under the light a man in his undershirt was seated at the kitchen table. He was reading the newspaper aloud to the woman while she cooked. As we appeared, the two of them were laughing about something he had just read. It was an ordinary scene in that neighborhood . . . almost.

My friend Chocolate was sitting about halfway down the stairs, holding a handful of pebbles. One by one he was dropping them through the boards of the step into the alley below. When we asked if he could play, he bounded up the steps into the kitchen, slamming the screen door behind him.

I watched as he spoke first to the woman at the stove and then turned to the man at the table. The man put down the newspaper, slipped his arm around the child, and pulled him close. Laughing, he said something we couldn't hear. He ruffled the child's hair and kissed him on the forehead. Then, shaking his head with a smile, he gave the child a gentle swat on the bottom as he ran back to the screen door. Slamming it behind him, Chocolate leaned over the rail and said something that sent my world spinning: "I can't play now. *My papa* says it's suppertime."

I stood in that alleyway a long time, rooted in the gravel, staring up at the picture of that kitchen framed by the screen door. I was frantically trying to phrase a question I had no words for. When I came to my senses, I realized that Zach was already around the big Packard and halfway to the cross street. I ran after him yelling, "Hey, Zach! Wait a minute, I . . ." But I never did ask the question.

You see, the woman at the stove was Chocolate's pretty mother. I knew her. She was black. But the man at the kitchen table, the man in his undershirt reading the newspaper to her, was a white man. I knew *him*, too. He didn't live in the garage apartment. Yet Chocolate had said, "*My papa* says it's suppertime" . . . *my papa*. Although I often puzzled over that statement, I never mentioned it to Chocolate, just as I never mentioned the mud pies. You see, there was a question welling up inside me. I kept struggling with it, but I didn't exactly know what the question *was*.

Summer soon ended, and Chocolate went back to wherever he lived with his grandmother during the winter to go to school. That fall we moved away from the neighborhood, and in December, Pep Herndon's great-grandmother died. I never saw Chocolate or his mother after that. Oh, once later, when I was a teenager I thought I saw him downtown with some other boys. I started to call out to him. But by then I knew that "Chocolate" was not an appropriate name for a boy, and I didn't know his real name. With a teenager's awkwardness, I decided not to speak.

The man I had seen sitting at the table that day was a different matter. I saw him often while I was growing up, and I knew him as

Mr. Vincent. I saw him coming and going from the bank. I saw him on the street corner talking business with other men. I knew Mr. Vincent was in the oil business with his brother in East Texas and that they owned large tracts of ranchland. The first time I heard the term "multimillionaire," it was in reference to Mr. Vincent. He lived not far from us in a large brick house with his pale, quiet wife. The Vincents weren't exactly part of the social scene in that town; they were just always *there*. They had no children. I saw Mrs. Vincent coming and going in the big, gray Packard or occasionally leaving the First Methodist Church. As a teenager I sometimes waited on her in the local department store where I worked. I never heard her speak above a whisper. She was always alone, and there was a kind of sadness about her.

Once, in my teens, I asked my father about Mr. Vincent. I wanted to know what kind of man he was. My father, who was never one to criticize, said, "I don't know a thing bad about Troy Vincent, except that he seems to be *his own worst enemy*." Only after I was grown did I realize that was a phrase my father reserved for people who had self-destructive habits—alcoholism, or compulsive gambling. But about Mr. Vincent, I never did know.

In time I grew up, went away to college, and never came back to live in that little town. From time to time, however, when my parents sent me letters, they included items of interest from the local newspaper.

One morning in Boston I pulled from my mailbox a letter fat with clippings. As I spread them out on the table, I saw the headline "Troy Vincent Murdered." I unfolded and read the rest of the clippings. Then I began searching for the obituary. I saw there were listed as survivors the pale wife, the brother in East Texas, and two nephews. No children were listed. There was no mention of my friend Chocolate.

It seems Troy Vincent had been found over half a mile from the nearest road in the middle of a pasture, stretched out on his back. He was wearing a three-piece suit, a white shirt, and tie—all neatly arranged. His arms were folded ceremoniously across his chest. There was a hat pulled all the way down over his eyes and ears. He had been shot in the abdomen at point-blank range with a shotgun. No weapon was found at the scene. There were no footprints, no clues. No one was ever apprehended for the murder. I thought about my friend Chocolate and wondered where he was.

Now, I'd like to tell you that his father sent him to Harvard Business School, made him a partner in his oil firm, and left him a fortune. The truth of the matter is, I don't know what became of him.

But one morning nearly twenty-five years ago, I was having breakfast with my husband, Pep Herndon (you remember—he was my childhood friend from across the street). Out of the blue, he wanted to know, "How well do you remember that bunch of kids on Third Street?" "Well," I said, "I remember some of them pretty well." He asked, "Do you remember a boy we called Chocolate?" Did I remember *Chocolate?!* I said, "Sure, I remember him." Next he wanted to know, "What was his name, really?" I blurted out, "I don't know what his real name was, but it *should've* been Troy Vincent, Jr." Pep stopped with his coffee cup in midair and stared at me for a long moment. When he finally set the cup down, he announced, "Well, I hope he's up to his elbows in oil wells, and he makes those old boys eat dirt."

Safety Pins and Polka Dots

WHEN I TURNED THREE YEARS OLD, IMPORTANT THINGS BEGAN to happen in my young life. First, on my birthday I got my ears pierced and tiny gold earrings inserted. Also, my formal education began—at Miss Nelson's School of Voice, Expression, Tap, and Ballet. That might have proven an expensive venture, but I'm sure some Depression-era bartering was involved. You see, my mother, the best dress designer in town, had just begun creating the costumes for Miss Nelson's little dancers.

I have always suspected that Miss Nelson was an unemployed showgirl when she came to town with her mother, a sturdy woman who played piano accompaniment for the tap and ballet classes. The two women rented a huge old frame house out on the highway. They lived on the second floor, while the great empty rooms on the ground level served as Miss Nelson's school. The wide expanse of bare wooden floors, the high ceilings, and tall, curtainless windows created a delightful echo chamber for the choppy rhythms of that out-of-tune piano, punctuated by the clickity-click of tap shoes.

I confess that I was not an eager pupil. A solemn, skinny child with lots of freckles and red hair, my long pigtails made me seem even more gangly and ungainly than I was. I had knobby knees and wore heavy orthopedic shoes laced snugly above my ankles. It must have been readily apparent to Miss Nelson that I was not destined to become a ballerina or an adorable tapping Shirley Temple. She must have known this even before she discovered that not only was I left-handed and left-footed, I didn't yet know which one was my *right* and which my *left* hand, or foot.

But in Miss Nelson's echoing parlor dance studio, I did learn some valuable lessons. The teacher's voice sometimes rose to a shrill pitch as she repeated, "Right foot, RIGHT foot, Rosy!" Her patience faded as I squirmed, gazing out the window instead of at her. Once she fairly screeched, "Your left hand side is toward the gas station, and your right side is . . . Do you know where the street out there goes?" I nodded solemnly. I had often ridden along that road on the way out of town with my parents. A gleam of instructional inspiration in her eyes, Miss Nelson cooed, "And *where* does the road go?" "To Abilene," I nodded confidently. "That's the way we go to Abilene."

She beamed. "Good. Now remember, your *right* side is toward Abilene, and your *left* side is toward the gas station." It worked. I remembered, until we did a shuffle and a half turn.

Later my big brother said she shouldn't have told me that. He said *east* was toward Abilene. And *west* was toward the gas station. To this day I'm somewhat directionally challenged.

Somehow Miss Nelson and I persevered. When my mother wasn't busy designing costumes, she conferred with Miss Nelson about choreographic effects. After a few months, they began to talk of a recital. As the event approached, my mother turned out design after design for teenaged dancers. The tallest boy got a red, white, and blue Uncle Sam suit. My favorite was a lacy fairy dress with silver toe shoes. There were green velvet elf suits and some blue ruffled dresses with twinkling stars for elementary-aged tap dancers. She even thought up costumes for preschoolers, like me.

Miss Nelson said I did a fine recitation of the verse about the little mouse, but that no, I wasn't going to dance a solo. I wouldn't get to dance any ballet numbers either, no matter how much I longed for a tutu and a pair of pink ballet shoes. Supporting her logic was the fact that I hadn't even graduated to the "pre-toe class," whatever that was. And I wouldn't take part in a speedy tap number wearing red satin shorts with a top hat and a walking cane. I thought those third and fourth graders looked so grown up, tipping their hats and twirling their canes—all except one girl, who seemed always to trip over her cane whenever she was required to twirl and tip at the same time.

My biggest moments in Miss Nelson's recital were to be two recitations during the first part of the program. In the second half of the program I would join two group numbers with other first-year dancers, all of us under the age of five. For the song and tap routine, Mother had invented a short, sparkly pile of stiff, shiny, purple-and-gold onionskin ruffles. She made mine as the prototype. I thought it looked wonderful, until I had to try it on and stand still *forever* while she pinned and repinned the ruffles. It was all scratchy inside. My big brother said I was learning to suffer for the sake of my art.

Our second group number was to be a sort of song and soft-shoe routine entitled "Comfortable Cats." It was composed and choreographed especially for preschoolers like me, allowing for our three-note singing range as well as for a degree of confusion about the distinction between right and left. I still remember the words.

My mother did herself proud with the required costuming for that routine. This time, however, she wasn't satisfied simply to make a prototype and a pattern for the other mothers to sew. To ensure uniformity, it was decided that she would make all the costumes herself. She made five little black cat costumes with little black feet fitted snug enough for dancing, small black mittens, and heads adorned with whiskers and perky ears. Only our faces showed. Each of us wore a big red bow at the neck and another at the *right* wrist, serving as a reminder in case we got out on the auditorium stage and forgot which way it was to Abilene. The most dramatic aspect of the costume was a long black tail with a horseshoe crook near the end, just long enough to brush the floor. My mother soon regretted that design.

She grumbled and fretted as she packed the stuffing into those long feline tails, using one of my father's golf clubs. Finally all five tails had to be attached securely to the costumes—by hand. Mother had made mine first, and I suspect she got better at attaching tails with each consecutive costume. Finally all were complete, rehearsals had ended, and the big night came. My mother removed my precious gold earrings before we left for the recital because Miss Nelson said shiny metal things glittered in stage lighting. I hated to appear at such an important occasion without my jewels, but nothing could have dampened my excitement to be taking the stage at the Municipal Auditorium.

First came the recitations. Each of us stepped out in front of the closed main curtain to "speak our piece." When it was time for the dancers, the curtains whooshed open to reveal a very little bit of set design, and we danced in front of the auditorium's only backdrop: a dense forest of tall fir trees lining a small stream of flat-looking water banked by symmetrical gray rocks. We children knew it was just a "made up" place. It certainly didn't look like anything we had ever seen in barren West Texas. The woodland fantasy had been created long ago by some traveling sign painter in need of quick cash, probably the same one who painted the River Jordan on the back wall of the baptistery at our church (same rocks, same water).

Our sparkly purple-and-gold tap routine was among the early dance numbers, and we did our best out there in front of the painted forest. Only one of our group had serious problems. Before we ever really started to tap, Darlene began to sniffle. Then, for no apparent reason, she suddenly emitted a loud wail, threw her stiff ruffly skirt over her face, and ran offstage. The clatter of her exiting tap shoes unnerved us all, but the wail that continued from backstage was soon interrupted by several insistent piano chords followed by an almost deafening introduction. The brave ones of us who remained heard "our music" and began the familiar steps. From the wings, Miss Nelson counted and coached more loudly than usual. We ended with a very nearly synchronized curtsy. Out front, our families applauded enthusiastically.

Once offstage, we were recostumed for our other big number. Actually we were sort of pushed into the costumes the way you'd stuff a pillow into a pillowcase. Then the five of us, black cats all, were placed on a large tumbling mat to keep our paws clean. The sitting still was hard, especially when surrounded by so much excitement. Big kids, brightly garbed, pranced onstage and off again, taking curtain calls. At last our three-year-old exuberance could be contained no longer. My friend Maxine stood up, reached around her chubby bottom, grabbed her long tail with one hand, and bowed from the waist as if the applause out front were all for her. We giggled. A loud "Shhhh!" came from behind a stretch of curtain, but it was too late. Already Nancy had leaned forward, flattened her cat ears against the mat, and turned a somersault. Her tail hit Margie in the face, rousing her to such an extent that Margie stood up and began kicking one leg wildly behind her to make the tail bounce. Soon all the preschoolers were on their feet, hopping up and down in imitation of the older dancers we had just seen clattering past. I ran a few steps forward across the mat and was brought up short. Some grown-up had taken a firm grip on my tail. Defiant, I lurched forward. But the tail didn't.

It wasn't a loud rip, just loud enough to bring Miss Nelson running. "No time for needle and thread," I heard someone say. She had me by the shoulder, and mumbled something about a safety pin. I was near tears. I had agreed to dance without my precious earrings, but without a tail, I certainly couldn't be a comfortable cat. So I turned bottoms up and endured the repairs and the scolding, hoping for the best. Miss Nelson wielded the safety pin, huge and new and shiny, and once or twice sort of stabbed me with it. To this day I'm not sure that was an accident.

Suddenly a group of dancers ran by for a curtain call, and Miss Nelson's shrill whisper ordered, "Line up here! Cat Number One, Cat Number Two, Cat Three . . ." We were out onstage. The piano pounded out the introduction. We posed over our "mats" and began singing shakily, "We are comfortable cats . . ." Of course, I wasn't. But it did seem to be going well—that is, until we turned our backs to the audience, stretched out in our most convincingly feline fashion, and stuck our bottoms up as we made a full turn. That's when I was faintly aware of a ripple of laughter coming from the audience.

Now, if you know anything about stage lighting and shiny objects, you will surely understand. What had been merely a large safety pin now shone in full glory as it caught the light, sending rays outward in all directions. On the second turn the whole audience began to chuckle. I didn't really understand until later.

My dance career was doomed from that day on. My mother said she had never been so embarrassed. She reminded me how hard she had worked on those suits, from ears to tails. And now her *own child* . . . It is a hard and heavy thing to be a family disgrace at such an early age. I bore that burden for several months until the following spring, when fate redirected it onto Jimmy.

My mother's baby brother, Jimmy, was graduating from high school. Like everyone in her family, Jimmy was musically gifted, and he had been chosen to provide the special music for the commencement celebration—a trumpet solo. The selection was "Carnival of Venice," a challenge for almost any high school trumpeter. He could play even the most difficult passages flawlessly and from memory. So, of course we all had to be there.

The entire family descended on my parents' tiny hometown for graduation weekend. On the day of our arrival, Jimmy and my mother, the family fashion consultant, went down to the local dry goods store to pick up his graduation suit (Mother had to approve the alterations). Oh, it was a handsome Palm Beach suit—just the color of vanilla ice cream. She treated him to a snappy pair of brown-and-white wingtip shoes to go with it. On the way out of the store they passed through the fabric department, an unfortunate turn, because my mother never could pass a display of fabrics without stopping to browse. While Jimmy waited, he shuffled through a counter stacked with fabric remnants. Suddenly something wonderful caught his eye. Delighted, he held it up and called, "Hey Sis, look at this!" The cotton remnant sported bright red two-inch polka dots on a white background. She laughed, "Now what would you do with *that?*" "Oh, you could make me some new boxer shorts! Wouldn't they be great? Please, Sis."

She finished the shorts before dinnertime, and on commencement day he wore them for the special occasion. He left for the dress rehearsal, proudly carrying his beautiful white suit on a hanger in one hand and his horn case in the other. He walked cautiously to keep his new shoes clean for his big solo. He was going to look splendid!

The family assembled at the auditorium early, to get good seats near the front. There was an entire row of us—my grandparents, all my aunts and uncles, my parents, and their children, all dressed in our Sunday best, of course, because we all knew how important it was to Mother that we appear in the proper attire.

The little graduating class marched in to "Pomp and Circumstance." The girls were all in white dresses, and the boys wore suits. The faculty and speakers filed onto the stage and sat in the front row of seats, while the honor graduates and my uncle Jimmy took the row behind them. He sat tall and handsome in his new white suit. From the audience, the whole family beamed. At last Jimmy's big moment came. He stepped forward, lifted his polished trumpet, and began to play magnificently. Beside me, my older brother, also a trumpet player, listened seriously as the difficult segments began. He was filled with admiration for his uncle. Then suddenly my sister nudged him in the ribs and squealed, "Oh, looky! You can see his underwear!" Someone in front of us noticed and giggled. Slowly others joined in, and soon most of the audience was attempting to stifle their laughter.

Our tall, proud musician played beautifully all the way through the triple-tongued passages, but the spectators barely heard it. They were far too amused by the sight of the huge red polka dots showing through the white trousers of the Palm Beach suit! My mother and her sister scooted down in their seats and ducked their heads. My father and the other men in the family struggled to keep straight faces.

My grandmother, never one to let propriety stand in the way of a good time, stifled a giggle. I was feeling really sorry for Jimmy. I knew how it must feel—or would feel, as soon as someone explained why the audience was laughing. But secretly I was also relieved because, as young as I was, I knew Uncle Jimmy had just taken over for me as the family disgrace.

The Wagon Trail

THE BUTTERFIELD-OVERLAND STAGECOACH LINE CAME INTO Texas from the Red River and curved westward, passing through Wise County. Francis Marion Barnett (named for Francis Marion, the "Swamp Fox" of Revolutionary War fame) and his wife homesteaded in Wise County along that trail in 1859, just before the Civil War. The Barnetts' daughter, Mary Frances Lucinda, married Henry Isaac Newton Scoggins. Henry's parents gave the newlyweds a wagon and team as well as other things they needed to begin farming on their own. The couple settled on their land, worked hard, and soon started a family with two little girls.

Part of their land needed to be cleared for planting, and one day while cutting and burning brush, Henry Scoggins was overcome by smoke. He seemed to recover, but a few days later he became very ill and died at only twenty-seven years of age (now we know that he had contracted pneumonia after inhaling the smoke). His parents then came and took back the wagon and team and all that they had given to the couple for their farm. Left with nothing, Mary Frances and the two tiny girls went back to live with her parents.

The older of those two baby girls was my grandmother Rosalie

Scoggins Woods. She and her sister grew up on their grandparents' farm, and everyone knew them as the "Barnett girls."

Rosalie's oldest daughter was my mother, who had fond memories of visiting the Barnett farm as a small child. When she asked her great-grandfather why he wore his hat brim pulled so low, he told her it was to shade his weak eyes. He said that during the war a powder flash from a muzzleloader had damaged his eyesight. He explained how he had marched away to war with the Wise County Confederate Company promising victory, and how he had returned home to his farm weary and defeated. Her Great-grandfather Barnett often told her stories about early life on his farm, encounters with friendly Indians, and the Overland Mail and covered wagon caravans that brought early settlers. He told her what it was like to come west by wagon. He said, "The early wagons and stagecoaches followed a trail all the way from the Red River right across this very land, right here where my barn and horse pasture are now." He continued, "When the first settlers crested a rise and saw the open, fertile land that was to become Wise County, they thought they had found the Promised Land."

Great-grandfather Barnett led her out across the farm once to show her a trail of deep ruts in the dry ground. She said she walked along in the indentations the wagon wheels had made, fitting her feet inside the grooved earth. He told her that this was the trail by which the covered wagons and stagecoaches had come west. With a child's logic, my mother deduced that, since the ruts disappeared at the top of a rocky knoll, that was where the trail west came to an end. For many years, she told her friends that the Butterfield Trail ended at the top of a hill on her great-grandfather's farm.

The Sound of Clocks

My mother's father was a country doctor, a tiny eccentric man who lived to be ninety-four years old. His often serious mood may have been meant to offset his slight stature. To me he was Grandpapa, but nearly everyone else called him Dr. Woods. Hardly more than a skeleton in appearance, he stood about five feet four, and he never weighed more than ninety-eight pounds in his whole life. He bought his clothes in the boys' department at Maxwell's Store. That long ago, there was not a wide variety of men's sizes. Still, he always dressed fastidiously. He emerged from his study for breakfast every morning wearing a three-piece suit with a well-starched white shirt and somber tie. I liked to see him bring out his round pocket watch, open it, and regard the time to be sure he was keeping to his strict schedule. He said knowing the correct time was important. He closed the watch with a light *click.* I liked the way it disappeared again into his pocket. I never saw Grandpapa dress to go outside or dress for a meal in any other way. But when he was back in his own study, he wore casual attire.

Now, casual attire consisted of "long-handled underwear." You know: long johns. So with Grandpapa, it was always either a white shirt with a tie and a three-piece suit, or it was long-handled underwear. There was never anything in between.

One Christmas during the Depression, my mother decided that my blue-eyed grandfather should be wearing pale blue dress shirts, as they were so much in vogue.

Now, locating just the right shirts in his small size proved challenging. My mother drove forty miles to a larger town and canvassed stores until she found them. Men's shirts were shipped to retail stores boxed by the dozen, so my mother bought her father an entire box of twelve beautiful dress shirts—all in fashionable pale blue. No matter that never once in his life had my grandfather been seen wearing a colored shirt. Even now a box of twelve shirts is an expensive gift, but in 1934 it was quite an extravagance.

Christmas Day came, and the living room floor was strewn with paper and ribbon. My mother brought over the present and set it before my tiny grandfather. Under its big red bow, the box of shirts looked enormous. We waited while Grandpapa removed the wrapping. He lifted the lid, ran his fingers down inside, and lifted the contents just far enough to see that all of the shirts were pale blue. He put the lid back on and slid the box across the floor in the direction of Uncle Todd, a six-footer. He said, "Here son, you can have these."

Mother was furious. She said, "What do you *mean*, 'He can have those'?" For a moment he paused. Then haltingly my grandfather explained: "I . . . I've had blue shirts before. They never did fit." For once even my mother was speechless.

Grandpapa also had a bit of trouble with his socks. At that time men wore garters around their legs to hold up their socks. But during World War II, no elastic was available for the garters. Still, a snappy dresser like Grandpapa wasn't about to go around with his socks sagging. His solution to the problem was to use the closest thing at hand: adhesive tape! Taking off his socks must have been an act of bravery.

In the little town where my grandfather lived, everyone had a favorite funny story about him. If I told people I was the old doctor's granddaughter, they were sure to tell me a good one. Many of those anecdotes centered around Grandpapa's driving habits.

He was such a poor driver that the mere sight of him coming down the street sent animals and small children scampering for the curb. He drove a big green Studebaker touring car that had remained unwashed since the day of purchase. The car had a windshield that folded down, and because the windshield was so dirty that it was no longer transparent, it was always folded down. That way, at least, he could see where he was going, though in Grandpapa's case, the seeing didn't have a close relationship to the going.

Every morning he followed this ritual: he took the heavy metal crank from the seat of the car, inserted it into the front, and turned the crank, until the car coughed and started. Then he tossed the crank over onto the front seat and hopped in. Looking straight ahead, Grandpapa slammed the Studebaker into reverse and backed out into the street. He then shifted gears and screeched forward, while the driver of any approaching car swerved wildly to avoid him.

When my youngest uncle, Jimmy, was a senior in high school, he had an important date—for the senior banquet, I think. He borrowed his father's car. To impress his date, he washed and waxed it. It glistened. None of us had ever seen it looking so bright a shade of green. Not only that, but the windshield was so shiny and clean that it was almost invisible.

The next morning when my grandfather came out, he took the crank from the seat of the car, walked around to the front, inserted the crank, gave it two or three good turns until the engine started, and then *tossed the crank right through the windshield.* We never knew what he was going to do next.

Once when I was downtown with my grandfather in that Studebaker touring car, he hopped out and told me to wait while he went into Dooley's Store for some red jawbreakers, his young patients' favorite candy. In a few minutes he came out, cranked the car, hopped into the driver's seat, and shifted into reverse. Then, looking straight ahead as he always did, Grandpapa gunned backward out of his parking space—straight into Mrs. Stratman's fine old Pierce Arrow automobile. My grandfather got out, surveyed what little damage there was, and remarked to a dumbstruck Mrs. Stratman, "Ahem . . . I guess it's OK. You can go on. I know you didn't mean to do it."

It was on his eighty-fourth birthday that I discovered that my grandfather was an extraordinary optimist. We had come out to spend that special day with him, and shortly after lunch he put on his hat and said, "I'm going downtown for a while." My mother said, "Where are you going, Papa?" "I have a real estate appointment," he said. She wanted to know, "Are you selling some of your rental property?" "No," he said, "I'm buying some." My mother, who always knew what everyone should be doing, asked, "What on earth are you doing buying more rental property at this time in your life? You're having trouble taking care of what you have now." Grandpapa's response was, "Well, if you must know, I'm buying it to take care of me in my old age."

Every visit with him was memorable. In that house, there were definite rituals about *time*. Dinnertime, for example. My grandmother served dinner precisely at 6:15 every evening. I used to wonder what would happen if someone had a medical emergency just then. But then I figured that no one would dare have an emergency when my grandmother was serving dinner in the dining room. Each person stood behind his chair, hands resting on the chair back, and waited until my grandfather appeared and pulled his chair out. That was the signal for the rest of us to be seated. Children arriving late for dinner got a silent look of reproach. My grandfather was always there at the head of the table before anyone sat. In unison, we bowed our heads, and he said grace. Although dinnertime always ran like clockwork, there were certain dinners I never will forget.

One sweltering Fourth of July at 6:15 p.m., we all stood behind our chairs, waiting for Grandpapa. But he didn't come. We waited, shifting our weight from one foot to the other. Grandmother fanned herself and looked toward the door. No Grandpapa. We returned to the living room and waited another half hour. Grandmother looked worried. My mother went to the telephone and called his office. She called the hospital. No one had seen him. Forty-five minutes passed. At last my mother called the town's central operator to ask, "Has anyone called for the doctor this afternoon?" There had been no calls. Finally, the children were fed, but the adults waited. After an hour had passed, even my father looked worried. He put on his hat and drove downtown. He returned to report that my grandfather's car was not at the office, nor was it in the parking lot at the hospital. My father had circled a few blocks and hadn't seen the Studebaker anywhere. It was eight o'clock now, the sun had set, and it would be dark soon. The adults went out to the front porch to catch a bit of breeze, if possible, on a hot summer evening. They looked up and down the street from time to time, but the children playing in the front yard were the first to see him coming. They yelled, "Grandmama, here he comes!" Grandpapa turned into the front yard and parked the dusty open touring car (it had no air conditioning, of course, unless there was a breeze). He got out and slowly walked to the porch. He looked not at all himself: Grandpapa was not wearing his coat! He was carrying both his suit coat and his tie. His vest was *unbuttoned*. He was drenched and obviously exhausted. Grandpapa dropped into the porch swing as my mother said, "Papa, we've been worried sick. Why didn't you call?"

He didn't answer, except to say, "May I have some iced tea?" He drained the glass, and after he had rested, this is the story Grandpapa told. It seems he had finished his rounds at the hospital. It was a holiday, and he had no appointments. He drove out to look at some billboards he owned (someone had told him they needed repainting). He said, "On the edge of town, I passed an old man hitchhiking in the hot sun. I felt so bad for him, that I stopped just to say I was sorry I couldn't give him a ride. But when I pulled over, he came running, tossed his old cardboard suitcase into the back seat and climbed into the car. With a big toothless grin he said, "Yes sir, Fort Worth!" I kept saying, "I'm sorry I can't give you a ride, old fella, because I'm only going a mile up the road." The hitchhiker repeated, "Yes sir, *Fort Worth!*" "You know," my grandfather said, "that old man was stone deaf." "What did you do, Grandpapa?" I asked. My grandfather leaned back in the porch swing and sighed. "I drove him to Fort Worth."

He was a softhearted man, but he didn't exactly know how to express what he felt for people. He refused to pursue collection of any past due accounts and sometimes paid for his patients' medications out of his own pocket. He would give away almost anything he owned. The only thing Grandpapa didn't share was the privacy of his study. At the back of the house, he sat at his big desk in a large bay window. That room was his undisputed domain. He sat there in his long-handled underwear, and if someone walked in he made no apology for his very casual attire because that was his place. The walls of that room were lined with books and clocks.

In the afternoons the dark green window shades were pulled down, protecting him from the sun's glare, and sheer panels softened the look to please my grandmother. The light filtering through those window coverings gave the room a slightly green glow. That room always had a musty smell of old book bindings and the unmistakable aroma of oil of wintergreen, his favorite flavoring for liquid remedies. To this day the fragrance of wintergreen or the sound of ticking clocks can transport me to that study.

Grandpapa collected antique striking clocks. At one time he had more than a hundred of them in that room, all ticking in different pitches. There were mousey ones that gave a skittering *tick-tick-tick-tick-tick-tick-tick,* and there were pendulum clocks that plodded through the minutes, authoritatively and methodically: *Tick. Tock. Tick. Tock.* Some were quick and cheery: *TICKtock! TICKtock! TICKtock!* One desk clock sounded like a little old lady in high heels hurrying across a wooden bridge: *ticktickticktickticktick.* When the clocks in my grandfather's study struck the hour, they struck in all different voices. But when they struck, they struck *all together.* If they didn't, Grandpapa leaped up to adjust them.

I was his favorite grandchild. I learned that I was because when I visited as a teenager, he would get out his violin and tune it to accompany me while I played the piano. It must have been a cause of concern for my older sister, who played piano much better than I did. But when Grandpapa tuned his violin and came to play with me, we could play only for twenty-eight minutes. Then we had to stop . . . to wait for the clocks to strike. If we had tried to play on through, we couldn't have heard the music.

I loved those clocks—the shape and luster of each case, and the steady swing of every pendulum, measuring the hours of the days in my grandparents' house.

As a very small child I often stood in the hallway to hear the clocks. My grandmother said grandchildren had to be *invited* into the study. It was not a place for children to play. Grandpapa was studying, she said. So I stood in the hall just out of sight and listened to the clocks. I thought they were the most wonderful sounds I had ever heard. I knew they were talking, about minutes and seconds and even hours, but they were talking to me about so many other things, too. In clock language. Maybe they knew how old I was, standing there. Had they been ticking that long?

One day when I was about four, I thought that if I could be very quiet, I could creep into the room to hear the clocks better. So very quietly, I crept over the doorsill and sat on the wooden floor. It was *wonderful*. The clocks stood all around me, some on shelves and tables, and the tall one, the Grandfather, standing near the door. I heard them say *ticktickticktickticktick* and *Ticktock, Ticktock, Ticktock*. Then they began to strike. What a marvelous noise! Some struck *BONG! BONG! BONG!* so that the very floor underneath me vibrated, and *ping!ping!ping!* and *Bingbong-Bingbong-Bingbong!* Amid all this commotion a bird woke up, popped her head out of a little wooden door, and exclaimed, *Cuckoo! Cuckoo! Cuckoo!* Then I must have wiggled because Grandpapa looked up from his desk and said, "Now, what are you doing down there?"

He got up from his chair and came across the room toward me. I thought I must be in terrible trouble because Grandmother had said children had to be invited. I said, "I was listening to your clocks, Grandpapa. I like your clocks." "You do, huh?" He looked surprised, and as he bent down I wondered what was about to happen to me.

He put one of his hands under each of my arms and lifted me right up into the air. Then, holding me way out in front of him, he carried me across the room and deposited me in a tall wooden chair, with my feet sticking straight out in front of me. He said, "If you sit there long enough, you can hear them again."

I sat in that chair a long time, and would sit there many times more, while he read to me from the *Encyclopedia Britannica* and from his medical journals. I sat there while he taught me to read *The Three Billy Goats Gruff*, and while he showed me how you could use the microscope to see the wonders of pond water under glass. That chair was my little acre in Grandpapa's private territory.

When I was eight or nine, Grandpapa wanted me to learn to paint. He thought I was artistic, like my mother, who painted pink and white roses on china. He had seen me with a coloring book once. He didn't approve of coloring books, and he had an odd way of getting that across.

One day he brought home a wooden case of oil paints. The beautiful colors lay in metal tubes next to the feathery brushes. He said, "I have this clock, uh . . . the glass broke. I've had the glass replaced, but there are supposed to be flowers on the glass. Would you paint a wreath of flowers around the face?" I said, "What kind of flowers, Grandpapa?" He said, "*Flowers*. Your mother's an artist—she must have taught you how to paint flowers!"

I painted flowers. And that was the beginning of one of the most frustrating days of my life. I painted flowers and wiped them off, and painted again and wiped them off, and painted again. Finally I showed him and said, "Grandpapa, what do you think about *these* flowers?" He said, "How do *you* like them?" "Well," I said, glancing at my work, "they're a lot better than the ones I did at first." His response was, "Looks all right to me. I think those will do." It wasn't until years later that I saw a clock like that one in a museum and knew how the flowers should have looked. Mine bore no resemblance.

Because I loved Grandpapa's clocks, and because I was his favorite, he taught me (and *only* me, of all the grandchildren) to wind them. He said, "Time is precious. Our lives are made of time, and the winding of clocks is a solemn obligation." The twenty-four-hour clocks we wound every evening. The eight-day clocks we wound on Sunday night.

During the last few years that my grandparents were alive, they needed a bit of extra attention. Every Wednesday morning I loaded my two small children into our station wagon and drove the hundred miles from Fort Worth to their house to do small chores and to relieve the tedium of their days. My two children always looked forward to going. Grandpapa sometimes showed them into his study. My son, Richard, in particular, had a seriousness that gave him a natural affinity for the clocks.

One day he and his sister spent a pleasant afternoon in the backyard picking up pecans. They had filled two baskets and a paper sack, and they greatly enjoyed displaying the heft of their collection. The next Wednesday the two of them could hardly wait to get there to pick up more pecans. As soon as we arrived they ran to the back door, grabbed the baskets, and headed into the backyard to look.

In just a few minutes they were back, looking heartsick. They wailed, "There aren't any pecans!" My grandfather, who by then was quite deaf, asked, "What are they saying?" I said, "Someone's picked up all the pecans, Grandpapa, and they were hoping to pick up pecans today." He said, "Wait just a minute till I get my hat."

He came back with all his suit pockets bulging suspiciously. Then the three of them went out "to take another look around." My grandmother and I watched from a window while he walked around the tree slowly, carefully dropping pecans from his pockets, then called the children over saying, "You didn't look over here!" Soon they were running and yelping. When they came in again they announced proudly, "When Great-grandpapa helps us, we find a lot of pecans!"

In my house there are five striking clocks. My favorite is a fine old Waterbury clock that sits on a shelf in my kitchen. Around the face of that clock, on the glass door that you open to do the important work of winding, is a wreath of flowers. It's rather crudely painted, but I wouldn't change it.

On the day we buried my grandfather, I walked through that old house with a great sense of loneliness. I heard from the study some small sound, and with a sudden burst of anger I thought, "Who dares?! Who *dares* go into that study uninvited?" I crossed the hall and stepped through the door to find my own son standing on that same straight wooden chair . . . solemnly winding his great-grandfather's clocks.

Different Grandmothers

MY OLDER SIBLINGS WERE GIVEN ORIGINAL NAMES, BUT WHEN I came along, a late-life surprise, my parents took their last opportunity to dispense a family name. To be evenhanded, they named me to honor both of their mothers, Rosalie and Christianna. The result was *Rosanna*. The name seemed a paradox to me. Maybe it destined me to become a woman of contradictions. Those two grandmothers were such different women.

Rosalie was pleased that I was named for her. She often spoke of it and said it created a special bond between us. But Christianna never mentioned the name, and I had no idea what she thought of it, or me, or for that matter what she thought about much of anything.

When summer came each year I was packed off to my parents' tiny hometown and turned over to the grandmothers. I could hardly wait to get there. My anticipation centered around Rosalie's house, but I faithfully divided my stay between the two.

However, I did think my maternal grandmother had an outdated code of etiquette. In conversation with people outside the family, she always referred to Grandpapa as "the doctor." I thought she did that because she didn't know his first name. So once, at about age four, I helpfully offered, "Did you know his name is Jesse?" My grandmother laughed and said yes she did, but that it wouldn't be proper for her to refer to him so casually among people who might be his patients. She said, "Do you remember how Mrs. Mandeville always speaks of her late husband?"

Oh yes, I remembered Mrs. Mandeville. She had a pointy nose and was profoundly deaf. She always wore the same navy crepe dress, with a pince-nez hanging from a shoulder pin. But what was most amazing about Mrs. Mandeville was her curved ear trumpet. To converse with her I had to wait until she held it up and then speak directly into its bell. Then I would jump back a little because she answered very loudly. She often said, "When my husband, Mr. Mandeville, was alive . . ." or "Mr. Mandeville, the mayor, used to say . . ."

To further her point, my grandmother added that her friend Mrs. Reynolds, the minister's wife, who stood next to her in the choir, referred to her husband as "the pastor," as in "The pastor and I went for a stroll in the park after dinner. He said it was a good place to recover after conferring with a disgruntled deacon." Even as a young child I knew that those women were part of a fading culture, but they were the most fascinating people I knew.

My mother's mother was a tiny, playful woman with an enduringly sunny disposition and a quirky sense of humor. When I asked why she was always so cheerful she said, "Oh, I guess the good Lord just gave me a funny way of seeing things, so I could live with your grandfather all these years." After I became a mother and considered that she had already outlived five of her eight children, three of them buried as young adults, I marveled even more at her lightheartedness. But by then I knew that it was the product of her indestructible faith in the wisdom of the Almighty.

No wonder everyone loved her. In town the grown-ups called my grandparents "Dr. Woods and Miss Rosy," but the children called them "Dr. Woods and Woodsie." I called her Woodsie, too, and knew that I shared her with dozens of other children who lived nearby. To them she was a fairy godmother with a bottomless cookie jar. As soon as a child stepped into her house, he knew he had entered a magical place filled with ornate things to look at and even hold, all presided over by a diminutive woman who adored children. If we ever mentioned her small stature, Woodsie would insist that she was really quite tall—taller than her own mother had been. She *said* she was five feet one. We all knew that was an exaggeration of at least an inch or more, but we let her pretend.

Woodsie was never too busy for children. Sometimes without notice she would stop right in the middle of housecleaning, turn off her noisy old vacuum cleaner, and say, "I just happen to have some little cakes, and if we made a few finger sandwiches, we could have a lovely tea party." She would remove her apron, go to the closet shelf, and take down a frilly hat stacked with big pink roses. Once it was perched jauntily on her head, the party was underway. The tea party was her way of teaching me how to behave appropriately at social events. I guess she expected my life to be an endless series of high teas. With her funny little chuckle, she demonstrated the proper form for introductions. "Miss Baby Darling," she would say to my doll, "may I present Mr. Theodore Bear. I've known Mr. Bear for years. We were old school chums, and you really must ask him to tell you about his days at Dartmouth." Then Woodsie would turn to me. "You must always remember to present the *gentleman* to the *lady*, and a young person to a grown-up." Sitting on a child-sized chair, she modeled for me a seamless blend of the pouring of tea and polite conversation while properly holding a small blue teacup.

Sometimes she would stop doing the dishes, dry her hands on a tea towel, and sit at the piano to teach me the hymn or folk song she had just been humming. In Woodsie's world, music and art were always more important than work, and children took precedence over everything.

Back in her sunroom there was always a colorful new appliquéd quilt in progress, for every young bride in town knew that her wedding present from Woodsie would be a quilt designed especially for her. My grandmother kept a list of people who had received her quilts, along with a description of each one. In time they numbered more than a hundred. She had so many original designs running through her head that to make them she had to work fast, not always worrying about the delicacy of the stitches. Vivid patterns were the reason her quilts came to life.

Maybe it was the way Woodsie sang in that lilting soprano while she stitched, but it seemed to me that the sun was always shining in that room. Sometimes we listened to radio soap operas and giggled together at their never-ending plots. One morning I brought my doll to the sunroom and plopped her down in the chair beside the quilt frame. Woodsie looked her over and commented, "Miss Baby Darling, your wardrobe is really quite inappropriate for a lady of your standing in the community." And she began to pull out fabric remnants and bits of lace and trim. We spent the rest of that day creating fashionable dresses for my doll: a pink checked dress with a white organdy pinafore, because pinafores were in vogue that year, and a blue silk dress with a draped neckline to wear to tea parties and "any wedding she might receive an engraved invitation to attend." We updated the hem on one of Baby Darling's older frocks and added an elegant touch of lace to soften the look. I was so proud of the stylish wardrobe, I couldn't wait for the invitations to arrive.

Woodsie made pretty dresses to surprise real little girls, too—Depression children who rarely had new clothes. In late summer she always turned out several. Since she lived directly across the street from the elementary school, on the first day of the school year she stood at her living room window and watched as those little girls arrived, smiling to herself as they entered, proudly wearing their beautiful new frocks.

All year long, Woodsie's house was open to children. She never locked her doors or latched the screen. Some child might want to come in for a cookie, to make a potty stop, or even to take refuge from a neighborhood bully. In the summertime, small athletes often limped in from the playground with skinned knees.

One summer at their house, I got sick. Tonsillitis, Grandpapa said. Woodsie had gone next door, the house was quiet, and I went to sleep on the living room sofa. When I opened my eyes, a small boy I had never seen before was standing in the middle of the room, his unblinking gaze fixed on me. "Hi," I croaked, and slowly sat up, holding my aching throat. He said solemnly, "Does Woodsie got any cookies?" I said, "I'm sure she does. Let's see." He followed me through the dining room into the kitchen. On the way he said, "I can have two." I knew then that he was one of Woodsie's regulars. I doffed the lid and held the jar down so he could choose. I said, "Yes, that's Woodsie's rule. You may have two." He took his time choosing and then turned toward the kitchen door. "What's your name?" I asked. His mouth already stuffed with a cookie, he muttered, "Jerome," and then went through the door and out the back gate. When Woodsie came home a few minutes later I said, "We had a cookie visitor. He said his name was Jerome." She just chuckled. It was such a common occurrence that she didn't even feel the need to comment.

I knew that during the school year a whole parade of children visited Woodsie. Grandpapa called them her "cookie brigade." Those visits were the highpoint of her day. I was always there when my school holidays allowed, and she taught me how to bake and serve cookies for our young guests. When school was in session, in mid-afternoon Woodsie seated herself at the piano, and hymns and merry tunes wafted out across the porch in the direction of Sam Houston School. From the front entrance of that school a path was worn through the grass all the way to the curb. Across Cherry Street the path picked up again and continued to Woodsie's front porch. Children who lived beyond Cherry Street never even considered following the sidewalk around the corner. The afternoon bell rang, and a stream of children followed piano music along the path straight through Woodsie's front door and back to the kitchen, where each one chose two cookies from the jar. They chatted for a moment with Woodsie and continued out the back door, through the gate, and down the alley to the next street. Along the way some waved to Mrs. Thomas as she took the laundry from her clotheslines, or peeped in the window of old Mr. Muir's workshop. Two or three of the children who had no one waiting at home sat at Woodsie's kitchen table or on a bench in the backyard for a glass of milk or Kool-Aid with their cookies. They filled Woodsie's ears with events of the day, and every one of them left smiling.

As I did, though sometimes reluctantly, when it was time to go to my other grandmother's house. On the established rotation plan, every two weeks of the summer I left that enchanted house of tea parties and formal dinners in the ornate dining room. Then I walked up an unpaved street to the edge of town to visit a very different house, and a very different grandmother.

My Grandmother Taylor's house was plain. It didn't even have a dining room. But it did have a huge kitchen with a bay window at one end, and a long table that seated eighteen people—twenty if we put two at either end.

You see, shortly after the First World War, my father's parents had decided it was time to move from the ranch into town so that their two youngest daughters could go to high school there. It was time for my grandfather to turn the heavy work over to younger men, and the new automobile made it possible for him to supervise from a few miles away. Moving to town didn't change their lifestyle much; they just brought it with them. Grandmother and Grandfather Taylor bought a large tract of land on the very edge of town—enough room for several horses, at least one cow and calf, and a huge garden plot. There was an assortment of poultry: chickens, turkeys, geese, a few guineas, and even some peafowl. They built a very simple house and in time added almost as many outbuildings as they had at the ranch.

By the time I came along, that was the size of things at the home of my widowed Grandmother Taylor, a tall broad-shouldered Scotswoman with a serious turn of mind who prided herself on her austere ways. Powerfully built, she was usually dressed in a plain cotton housedress with a white canvas apron wrapped all the way around her ample waist and tied in front the way the butchers in the stores at home wore theirs. Her white hair was pulled up tightly into a no-nonsense knot on top of her head, but during the day her curly hair would break loose and make a fringe of little white ringlets around her face. I liked her curls. They softened her. Once I teased, "Grandmother has curlicues!" A stern look came over her, and a few minutes later I saw her in front of the bedroom mirror with a wet comb, fiercely slicking those stray curls back against her head. She permitted herself no vanities. In contrast to the giggling, childlike Woodsie, it was hard to imagine that my father's mother had ever been a child.

Grandmother Taylor always seemed to be immersed in hard work—gardening, caring for animals, and cooking. The kitchen was the heart of that house, and I knew she was never happier than when every place at the table was filled with her rowdy brood and their families. Two lived nearby, and all eight of them came for every holiday and often for weekends. They were always there when there were fences to mend or cattle to work at the ranch, and when there was canning to be done. Her children were all as strong and as tough as she was, but I have never known a family who had more fun just being together. They all pitched in, but no matter how hard and dirty the work, there was such friendly competition and so many jokes and pranks that even work became great fun. No matter how long the work day, at night they would set up two card tables in the living room and play 42 or dominoes and cards until far into the night, laughing and joking long after their mother had gone to bed. I wondered how a serious woman like herself had raised such fun-loving children.

Sometimes when we visited in wintertime, Grandmother's quilt frame would be out in the living room. It was suspended from hooks and could be pulled up against the ceiling out of the way when visitors came. My mother always asked to see the quilt in progress. Unlike Woodsie's bright designs, Grandmother Taylor's quilts usually had quiet colors. The curves of the quilted lines were flawlessly even, "stitched to last," she said. My Uncle Roy said they were just "hell for stout." Once the family convinced Grandmother to enter one of her more colorful sunburst quilts in the county fair, but the judges disqualified it because they thought it had been pieced on a sewing machine. Grandmother was furious and never entered *anything* in the fair again. Although it was a subject my father said was best left unmentioned, I understood why the judges had been fooled. I had often examined the quilts on the bed where I slept and marveled at the fine, perfectly stitched rows. I even tried to spread the seams enough to see a thread or two. I never could. They were too tightly sewn.

In summer, I usually arrived at Grandmother's in the evening. When I was ready for bed, she would appear in the bedroom doorway and say quietly, "Evening prayers, child." And I would drop silently to the kneeling rail at the foot of that tall bed. After I said "amen," I'd climb up on a chair and jump as high and wide as possible, sinking down into the deep feather bed. She always tucked me in. Then I'd listen to her heavy footsteps on the bare floor as she went up the hall. I would have known those footsteps anywhere. They were uneven, the rolling gait of an old woman whose hip joints were worn out. Then I dozed off to dream of floating aloft on a cloud of feathers and down, where angels coveted my grandmother's sparkling white sheets and her finely stitched quilts to make their robes.

The next thing I knew, Grandmother would be calling, "Rosy, oh Rosy, you go'na sleep all day?" I'd fight my way out of that feather bed and hit the floor, grabbing for my clothes. *It must be nearly noon!* Then I'd see the clock: 6:30. That was as late as she ever let me sleep. She had been up since 4:00 looking after animals and cooking a big breakfast that would have fed a half dozen hungry ranch hands. There were eggs and big, fluffy biscuits with sausage and ham, or steak and bacon. Always there was oatmeal—porridge, as she called it. And she ate it the Scottish way, with salt. I suspected that some mornings at 4:00 she went out to the henhouse in the pitch dark and snatched some poor fryer off the roost before he could even open his eyes because there on the breakfast table would be fried chicken, cream gravy, and thick, crusty, batter-fried potatoes. All prepared before I awoke.

Once Grandmother asked me what I ate for breakfast at Woodsie's house. I said, "I usually have Post Toasties." She wanted to know what they were: "I never bought any. What are they?" But the next time I came, she had a box. She looked suspiciously at the flakes as she poured a bowl for me. I turned away for just a moment and then turned back again to find that she had put a big spoonful of thick cream on top of the cereal. It just sat there. I tried to stir it in, but the cereal and cream all just balled up in the middle of the bowl like a popcorn ball. She couldn't believe people ate the stuff with runny milk. So, morning after morning one plump, elderly woman and a skinny little girl sat down at one end of the long table with black coffee and huge goblets of milk to go with the kind of breakfast she considered appropriate preparation for a day's work. No tea parties and finger sandwiches here.

With breakfast cleared away, Grandmother went to the wall hooks in the back hallway, took down her big sunbonnet and a smaller one for me, and we were off to the garden. I couldn't understand why Grandmother Taylor worked so hard to grow all that produce. I don't know the dimensions of her garden, but years later it provided sites for three rental houses and their yards. The rows seemed to go on forever, always with more to hoe and a lot to pick. Okra and squash, beans and peas, potatoes and corn. She even grew celery. We filled baskets and pails with ripe vegetables. By midmorning I was dragging my feet, and she let me make a trip to the house to take a pail of produce and bring back drinking water. On my way back to the house I sometimes wished I were back at Woodsie's. At *her* house I would probably have been sewing doll dresses or learning a new song at the piano by this time of day. So to make the morning more fun, I hummed one of Woodsie's cheery little tunes and munched on a few cherry tomatoes from the top of the pail. Their ripe, sun-warmed flavor was one of the best things about working in that garden. But Grandmother Taylor never slowed, never quit or complained, although summer by summer she hobbled with greater and greater difficulty up and down those long garden rows. When the sun was high overhead, she would remove her bonnet, mop her face with a big handkerchief, and say, "We'll eat now, child." We hauled our pickings up to the house for "a real noon meal."

Once while we ate I said, "Grandmother, why do you have such a big garden? One little plot near the house would grow all you can use." All she said was, "We need fresh vegetables." I thought it was poor planning. The worst over-production I had ever seen, in fact. I couldn't fathom why she drove herself so. Why, even I could see that if she grew less, she wouldn't have to do all that canning. Every year she canned a cellar full of fruits and vegetables and ended up giving it all away. Some went to her children but most to the women who lived along her street. But I knew to keep my views to myself.

After lunch, while we rested from the heat, we did what she called "light chores," like sweeping and mopping floors, or baking. The time I liked best was when she sat in the big bay window and churned. I loved the rhythmic sound of the wooden dasher thumping up and down in the big crockery churn. When she started working the butter, I knew there would be shortbread. Oh, not that stuff that comes in little tin boxes. *Real* shortbread. While the butter was still soft, she dipped a paddle full and plopped it into a bowl. When she had finished working up the butter, she came back to the bowl to add other ingredients—sugar, flour, and vanilla. Then she would press it all into a round pan and slide it into the oven with whatever else was baking. Her shortbread wasn't a dessert, and not exactly a cookie either. It just sat on a plate at the back of the stove so we could break off big chunks to munch on while we worked around the kitchen.

How that woman could cook! I tried to learn from her, but for directions she said things like, "Add sugar until you think you have enough." Once I asked her to teach me to make a molasses cake I liked. She said, "I'll just *make* one." I ran for a pencil and notepad. I should have known she didn't have a printed recipe for anything. I watched her dump in ingredients and scribbled notes, trying to keep up. I said, "Wait, wait—how much flour was that?" She tilted the bowl in my direction and said, "About that much." When I asked how much molasses she was going to add, she finally gave me a precise answer: "Four gullops." "Four *what*, Grandmother?" She said, "Listen, child." She tilted the jug and let the thick syrup pour out over the mound of flour: *gullop, gullop, gullop, gullop*. She set the jug down and said, "That's about right."

Her pies and cobblers were especially good. One of my favorites was a winter pie, a fresh lemon cobbler that I never ate anywhere but at her house.

With baking in the oven, we went out to work again. Sometimes we would work her roses because she knew I loved them. My grandmother said, "Lawns are for city people." And from the hedge that marked the boundaries of the yard on three sides to the wide front porch, there were rows and rows of rosebushes. She never cut the roses for the house. But she did sometimes cut armloads for a sick friend in the hospital. Grandmother Taylor grew things, and the roses were the least practical thing she occupied herself with. Roses and a few peafowl.

One day when I was still small, I admired a strutting peacock and ventured too close. He took a hop, turned, and began to chase me. Terrified, I went tearing through the maze of that rose garden, dodging and darting here and there, and finally scrambling up the front porch steps to find her standing at the railing. She was laughing her rare funny laugh that made almost no sound. She would tuck her head and simply shake from head to foot. At times like that, or when I did something foolish, I have heard her turn quietly to a friend and say, "Her mother is a town girl."

In middle to late afternoon, when we went into the kitchen for a glass of cold water or iced tea, I would choose an apple from the bowl on the big, long table. At home I would have eaten a whole apple for a snack, but not here. I would bring the apple to her and say, "Grandmother, may I have half an apple?" She knew what I wanted, and her eyes twinkled. She would grasp the apple in her two big hands and give it a mighty twist. I'd hear the apple *rip* and then she would hold out before me two evenly divided apple halves.

When I went back home to school in the fall, sometimes I would eat an apple in the lunchroom. I would hold up the fruit and say to my friends, "My grandmother can twist apples like this right in half." And they would say, "Oh, that's a big fib. Nobody can do that." "Well my grandmother can," I would say, "but I'll bet *your* grandmother can't do it."

The best part of the day at her house was when the milking was done and the evening meal had been cleared away. Grandmother would take her mending basket and needlework, or a pail of beans to snap or peas to shell, go out to the front porch, and take her seat. Something about the way she settled herself into that chair always reminded me of the way Woodsie seated herself at the piano in the afternoon just before the school bell rang. I had the same feeling of anticipation. I perched on a railing to wait. As soon as Grandmother sat down, they began to appear.

Women emerged from their houses one by one, as a whole neighborhood of elderly widows came along the street to the Taylor house. They all carried something. Some came with knitting bags or baskets. Some were returning empty bowls or plates. One walked along swinging an empty milk jar by the bail. They came through the rose garden stopping once or twice for an appreciative whiff, until at least six or seven women lined the front porch to "sit a spell."

Some did needlework and others joined in the pea shelling or bean snapping. They chatted in soft, old lady voices, and I liked to listen to their stories. There was Mrs. Tate, Mrs. Smith, Allie Brown, and Bessie Landers. And there was one ancient, paper-thin woman everyone called "Aunt Dody." She wasn't any taller than I was and always had snuff stains around her nearly toothless mouth. I helped bring out pitchers of tea and cold milk, sometimes with cookies or cake. Aunt Dody always had milk. She would often say, "This cold sweet-milk sure is good, Annie. Now if'n it was some cold biscuits or cornbread in it, it'd be purely perfect." Grandmother would nod to me, and I'd go in to put biscuits or chunks of cornbread into a goblet with more milk and a spoon for her. Aunt Dody always sighed contentedly and said, "I thank you, dear."

As darkness fell and made work impossible, Grandmother said, "We picked okra and squash today," or "We have a world of cucumbers this year. Could you use some? How about some of these peas or beans?" I followed her with her rocking gait, through the now darkened house to the lighted kitchen, to help fill baskets or paper bags with fresh vegetables. She added in other things like jars of jelly, canned fruit, or fresh loaves of bread, and wide-mouthed jars of homemade soup. In Aunt Dody's basket she put chunks of cold cornbread and other extras. She would call from the kitchen, "Aunt Dody, can you use some milk?" To all she would call, "My hens are laying really well. I'll send you off with some eggs." When we brought the baskets out, she would say, "My peaches are ripe. I put in a few. No need to let them go to waste." I saw her do this hundreds of times. But I didn't really *see*.

I knew that my grandmother's house was the gathering place, a center of social activity, but not until I was older did I see that she had fed a whole neighborhood of Depression-era widows. I'm sure she never thought of herself as having a mission, but she had one.

When oil came in across that ranch, it didn't change her lifestyle any more than the move to town had. All the money meant to her was that she could buy any new rosebush that caught her eye in the seed catalog. She still got up at 4:00 and though she hobbled with more and more difficulty, she worked those long garden rows in chill and heat, as if it were a matter of life and death. And for some in that town, it may have been.

She never stopped. She never complained. She taught her children and her grandchildren how to work, and that work was about more than just meeting our own needs, or supplying our frivolous wants. She showed us how to take care of people who needed our help without robbing them of their dignity. Those who entered her house may not have been greeted with playful tea parties or lilting music, but they found the same spirit of hope and a quiet generosity without the slightest trace of condescension.

I have always known I looked a bit like my Grandmother Woods. I identify with her in more ways than just the "Rose" part of our names. And while in time, my own children loved going to Woodsie's house as all children did, for me the scent of roses always calls to mind a different grandmother and a front porch filled with the sound of old ladies' voices. Now some days my own footsteps even sound a bit like my Grandmother Taylor's, and as I grow older I think more and more of that strong old Scotswoman. How I wish I could talk to my Grandmother Taylor now. I'd like to tell her I make pretty good shortbread and that I finally mastered her fresh lemon cobbler, after more than a decade of trial and error. But I never could make the molasses cake; I guess I never got the gullops right. Most of all, I wish I could tell her that now I understand about the garden.

Seeing Ghosts

My mother was not really a storyteller. This is one of the few stories I heard from her.

My parents, Eula Woods and Richard Taylor, had known each other all their lives, and when they married shortly after World War I, both were working at the railroad depot. Eula, a tiny woman of five feet two inches, who weighed no more than ninety-seven pounds, worked in the telegraph and ticket office, and Richard, who stood well over six feet, was the freight depot stationmaster.

Sometimes Richard had to work at night, and when he did, Eula took her needlework and went to her parents' house a few blocks away and visited until they went to bed. Then she walked out the back door and along the tracks to the depot to meet her husband, so they could walk home together.

That little town where Eula had grown up was the safest place on earth to her, especially since she had gone away to school in the city of Fort Worth. Now she was happy to be back where she knew every inch of town and everyone in it. By moonlight she could walk with confidence from her parents' back door past the garden and the cow lot, around the boardinghouse, and along the path through vacant lots to the railroad tracks. From there she turned west at the foot of Watertower Hill, where she followed the tracks to the lighted depot. Richard would be watching for her from the window above the freight desk, where he stood finishing up his paperwork. She knew as soon as he saw her he'd grin and say, "*Here's* my girl!"

One night she put her basket of needlework over her arm and headed along that path to meet Richard just like she always did. The full moon cast a strong light, and just as she approached the tracks, Eula noticed a fiery glow off the east end of Watertower Hill. She crossed the tracks and hurried along another path to see what might be burning over there. She expected to see a grass fire. She heard voices, and as she rounded a curve in the path, she saw in front of her a gathering of men in white robes and hoods. They were walking toward her. She realized the fiery light came from torches held high. The Klan!

In terror Eula jumped off the narrow path and ducked behind a cluster of thick bushes. She crouched in the dark, afraid to move. She clutched her sewing basket to her chest—maybe it would muffle the pounding of her heart. Everyone in town knew that her papa had no use for the Klan. She knew what they were capable of, and she didn't want them to mistake her for a spy. The hooded figures chatted and joked among themselves as they came along the path single file. Eula tried not to breathe. As each man passed, his white robe brushed against the bush where she was hiding. Trembling, she struggled to hold still, and she began to recognize the voices. In a flash she thought, "These Klansmen are men I've known all my life!" She heard Fred Jackson who ran the hardware store, Howard the blacksmith, Mr. Clark who passed the collection plate at church, Edgar Smith the butcher. She heard the unmistakable bass voice of old Oscar, who worked at the wagon yard where her in-laws stopped when they came to town. There was John from the icehouse. Clyde, a former classmate, who worked at the feed store. Oh . . . even her friend Martha's new husband, Ben . . .

After the procession had passed, Eula waited a long time to be sure they were completely out of sight. Still trembling, she stood and headed up the railroad tracks at a dead run, toward the lights of the depot. As she hurried through the door Richard said, "*There's* my . . . What's wrong, sweetheart? Have you seen a ghost?"

Eula began to cry. She whispered, "Yes, a whole string of them, in white robes."

He came around the desk and put his arm around her.

"Did they see you?"

"I hid, but I was *so* scared," she sobbed.

Richard drew her closer and planted a kiss on the top of her head. "Well, no ghost would want a little bitty thing like you."

Eula tried to laugh while Richard dabbed clumsily at her tears with his handkerchief. She sat on a bench near the desk and waited while he closed the freight office for the night. Then he took her hand and held it securely all the way home. But the whole town seemed different to her somehow, and when she walked alone at night forever after, she was always just a little bit on the lookout for ghosts.

Panhandle's Coming!

West Texas has always been a windy place, and all too frequently it endures a sustained drought. Drought always reminds me of the Great Depression and the period that became known as the "Dust Bowl Days." I am a native West Texan, and I grew up during that era when water was so scarce that local laws forbade washing automobiles or watering lawns. It seemed that the dry wind was always blowing, *but I have never seen a dust storm.* No, I'm not preparing for a liars' contest. Let me explain.

My little hometown has never had much to boast about. Shortly before I was born, writer Dorothy Scarborough chose our town as the setting for a novel. It was appropriately titled *The Wind.* Residents of that town didn't brag about the book. In fact, they resented it. They felt it reflected unfavorably on the town. "Why, the whole story is preposterous," they said. "The very idea that the wind and blowing dirt could drive a person mad!"

About the only thing the town could boast about was the world's largest gypsum plant. It was known locally as "the gyp mill." You probably know that gypsum is a white chalky mineral used to make wallboard. In other places, gardeners buy it in small bagfuls and stir it into flowerbeds to loosen the soil. Our soil was heavy with gypsum. One of the first jokes I remember hearing was about a tourist who stopped at a local service station and said, "Our travel guide says you have the world's largest gypsum plant. We sure hope we've come at the right time of year to see it in bloom." Even now, when travelers drive through the area and see the iron-red soil, they often assume it is clay. It isn't. It's loose, gypsum-laden sand.

Now, sand plus wind plus drought equals *sandstorms*, not "dust storms." In dry periods before erosion-control efforts began, that red sand was always airborne. It blew up in drifts along roadways and fencerows. It ground the paint from wooden houses and barns and drifted against buildings, leaving rusty red stains along the lower halves of their masonry walls. The wind-driven sand gave rise to everyday housecleaning rituals that every West Texas woman knew.

I learned the rituals when I was quite small. At our house everyone had chores, and long before I was old enough to go to school, I helped with meal preparation. Following the ritual before every meal, I removed the crystal bowl from the center of the dining room table and the lace tablecloth underneath it. I wiped the bowl with a clean cloth, and dusted the table. I covered the table with a fresh linen cloth before setting the table with dishes and silverware. When the meal was over and the dishes were all taken away, I removed the linen cloth and replaced the lace cloth and bowl. Three times a day the ritual was repeated. I grew up thinking that mothers and daughters the world over dusted their dining tables three times a day. Once when I was about eight or nine we visited relatives in East Texas. In an effort to be helpful, I offered to dust and set the dining table. My offer was taken as an insult to our cousin's housekeeping. She said her dining table didn't *need* dusting!

We observed other complex rituals related to blowing sand when we did laundry. Some mornings, even before I opened my eyes, I knew it was Monday, laundry day. I could hear the unfamiliar sound of running water coming from a garden hose attached to the faucet outside my bedroom windows. The hose ran across the yard to our laundry room, filling three well-scrubbed washtubs with cold water. The galvanized tubs sat on stands in a cloverleaf arrangement with the washing machine. That electric machine, the envy of my mother's friends, was waiting to be filled with scalding hot suds. Wash day had already begun.

I dressed quickly. The important business of the day was already underway. In the back hallway I could see that the water heater was turned up to its hottest setting, with the gas flame burning beneath the tank. One end of another garden hose ran in through the back door and was attached directly to the drain faucet of the heater. I stepped over the hose on my way into the kitchen. Breakfast was a hasty affair on washdays. The big pot of starch cooking on the stove overruled the usual skillet of bacon and eggs. More temperamental than cream gravy, that starch had to be stirred constantly with a long wooden spoon to avoid lumps.

In the laundry room, the round washing machine's green enameled tub stood up on legs, and the gyrator made a distinctive sound as it moved forward and back in quarter circles. That wonderful machine had a powered wringer—you didn't even have to crank it! By the time I was out of bed, the long hall that ran through our house was stacked with several large piles of carefully sorted linens and clothes waiting to be laundered. The heap nearest the back door consisted of men's white shirts, table and bed linens, and dresser scarves. Those things went to the machine first, to be washed in the hottest, soapiest water. The next stack up the hall was made up of underwear, school clothes, and towels, followed by the boys' khaki pants and heavy darker-colored things. Each pile waited its turn.

Every piece of laundry was inspected, and spots or stains were given a hand scrubbing on a rub board with lye soap and even bleach, if needed, before being dropped into the gyrating tub. When a machine load had run long enough to be judged clean, my mother wielded the "punching stick." The stick was an eighteen-inch section from a broom handle. Long ago the paint had been washed away, and the whole stick was bleached white after years and years of laundry days. The midsection was worn thinner than the rest. That's where steamy hot laundry was dipped up from the machine and fed through the ringer into the first tub of clean rinse water. Then the next stack from the hall went into the still-hot suds. In preparation, the ringer was rotated past the first rinse tub. The first load was rinsed up and down by hand and passed through to the next tub, until it had been rinsed in three tubs of water. Finally, each load went through the ringer into a clean, dry tub. Using that automatic ringer had to be done cautiously so that fingers weren't grabbed and mashed flat along with the fabric. My mother set the warm boiled starch near the dry tub, and shirt collars and cuffs were carefully dipped. Now, one by one, the heavy tubfuls of wet laundry were ready to be carried to the backyard clothesline.

Mother, or one of my older siblings who was tall enough, wiped the long metal clothesline with a damp cloth to clean away the red sand before anything was hung. My job then was to hand up wooden clothespins to those tall people who would clamp the pins tightly to each piece as it went carefully onto the line. I knew that the pieces must never be allowed to drag in the dusty grass below the lines. Heavy, wet sheets were folded double for hanging, and shirts were pinned to the line by their tails, with long sleeves left to blow free in the breeze. A housewife wouldn't think of hanging dingy shirts and linens, since the rows and rows of snowy whites were left flapping in the wind for all the neighbors to see. My mother inspected the laundry as it was hung to protect her reputation as a fine housekeeper. Soap commercials on the radio told women they must never be guilty of hanging out a wash that was "tell-tale gray" or shirts that tattled "ring-around-the-collar!" When every inch of the clothesline was heavy with wet clothes and linens, my mother would back up and nod with satisfaction for just a moment before going back to rotate the next tubful to completion. In the West Texas wind, the laundry dried quickly, and when all went well, by late afternoon the clothes could be gathered off the line like ripe fruit from vines, then carried into the house and loaded onto a bed where towels and sheets could be folded. Everything else was sprinkled lightly to dampen it a bit and then rolled into tight bundles and wrapped in a quilt to wait overnight for ironing. Nobody had ever heard of wrinkle-free fabric, and Tuesday would be ironing day. When I climbed into bed at the end of a busy laundry day, the crisp white sheets smelled like fresh air and sunshine. The aroma lulled me to sleep. Now, that's how it worked when all went well.

But sometimes it happened—the one thing that my mother dreaded most on laundry day. When the lines were full of beautiful clean clothes and linens bleaching in the sun and snapping in the wind, we looked off toward the northwest to see that the whole sky was no longer blue. It was *brown*, and a heavy bank of dark, red-brown clouds was rolling in fast from the Texas Panhandle. The one who saw it first sounded the alarm. To this day, I can hear my mother frantically shouting, "Sandstorm!" At the sound of those words, the whole family would spring into action. We were well trained in sandstorm emergency procedures. Anyone tall enough to reach the clothesline headed to the yard at a dead run to grab as many of the damp items as possible and get them into the house before the sand hit. We sometimes joked that on those days most of the topsoil from the Panhandle blew past us, and when my teenage brother sounded the alarm, he always yelled, "The Panhandle's coming!"

I wasn't tall enough to reach the clothesline, but I knew my job when the alarm came. Speed was all-important. With my heart pounding, I ran upstairs as fast as my short legs could go, to the northwest corner bedroom. I started there, grabbing the handles of every open window and tugging hard to slam it closed. Sometimes those tight wooden frames stuck, and I had to swing from the handles with my whole weight to bring the window down before moving on to the next one, until every upstairs window was closed and locked. Then I ran downstairs to begin the process again in the northwest corner of the living room. I couldn't slow down. I knew any minute the grown-ups would come scrambling into the house, searching for places to hang wet laundry to dry indoors.

Sometimes, if the alarm was sounded late, or the team was slow, the beautiful white sheets and other laundry were stained with rivers of thick red mud—a long day of hard work completely ruined. I have seen my weary mother weep at the sight. That meant tomorrow wouldn't be ironing day; it would be washday all over again.

No matter how the day had gone, ruin or success, before dinnertime there was still more work to be done. The washing machine and the tubs had to be emptied and cleaned. No longer clear, that tired, murky water was still too precious to waste. My mother dipped it out into buckets until the tubs of water were light enough to lift. Then, by the bucketful, by the tubful, that slightly soapy water was hauled into the yard to pour under trees and shrubs in a desperate effort to keep vegetation alive until the drought ended.

As a result of erosion control, irrigation of Panhandle farmland, and climatic changes, we rarely see serious sandstorms anymore, even during dry years, but my heart still races a bit at the memory of that shout: "The Panhandle's coming!" Now, I appreciate my automatic laundry equipment, but sometimes I climb into bed at night between sheets just out of the dryer, sheets that have never been bleached by the sun or dried in the blowing wind, and I miss the delightful fragrance of fresh air and sunshine.

The Song

One day in church we were singing something like "Oh God, our help in ages past / Our hope for years to come, . . ." and I watched my mother and father holding a hymnal between them. For the first time I noticed that while my mother was singing, my father was only speaking the words. Later, as the congregation poured out onto the steps of First Baptist, I asked, "Daddy, how come you didn't sing the hymns?" He answered simply, "I can't sing." He said that all *he* could do was make a joyful *noise*.

"But why can't you sing?" I insisted.

"I guess I just don't know how."

So, with the full gusto of my six years, I volunteered to teach him.

After dinner I got my father to go to the living room with me. He stood by the piano while I played the scale. I insisted, "Now, hum after me: Do, re, mi, fa, so, la, ti, do!"

My father chanted back solemnly, "Humpti-humpti-humpty, humpty-hump." All of the *humps* were executed on about the same pitch. Not a bass or a baritone, Daddy was decidedly a monotone. Exasperated, I had him try again and again, to no avail. My mother and older sister as well may have attempted to give my father voice lessons, with about the same effect. Though he pretended to be a willing pupil, he really could not sing.

It was for this reason that our family so enjoyed Daddy's telling of one story in particular from his days in a field artillery unit during World War I.

"We were somewhere in France, near the end of the war," he would begin. "At roll call I heard my name called among a group of men ordered to report for a bus trip, and I didn't know why. But it sounded better than being hunkered down by a 155-millimeter gun all day, so I reported anyway. The people boarding that bus were all strangers to me, so I asked the man next to me, 'Where are we going?' With a smirk on his face he said, 'Oh, you know where we're going. This is the trip to Paris.' Well I had been on the front for so long that being anywhere else sounded just great to me. Besides, I hadn't been to Paris. I decided just to keep quiet and enjoy the trip, *wherever* we were going.

"As we drove through the countryside we saw shattered villages and the ruined fields of small farms. Along the road, country women stopped their work to wave and smile. Some called out, 'Americans, Americans!' Behind us, we could still hear the big guns. The rumbling faded as we rode along, but we were way down the road before that sound was completely gone. When it stopped, the silence was overpowering. It had been months since I had enjoyed real silence. It was like country silence, like the silence out on our ranch, a kind of quiet that made me think of home.

"On the outskirts of Paris we were excited to hear horses and teams, delivery carts and ice wagons, and people calling out to each other. The sight of a pretty girl walking along the street brought the entire busload of soldiers to the windows. We waved and called to her until she was out of sight.

"Finally the bus unloaded at a reception hall. We all just stood there and stared—there were crystal chandeliers overhead and long tables with white linen tablecloths! In a minute someone showed us to our seats, and they served us a lavish meal. Suffice it to say, that bunch of hungry old soldiers had eaten very few warm meals. Supplies had been scarce for months. The whole scene was almost too good to be true. I kept wondering why we were here, but it didn't squelch my appetite any. I dug my fork into the French cuisine and thought, *So far this Paris trip has turned out even better than I'd hoped!*

"After we ate, we boarded the buses again. After a short ride, we stopped at an imposing building where gargoyles glared down from the edge of the roof. I stepped down and fell into formation with the troop. Two abreast, we marched quickly through a door. We passed a huge, curved staircase banked by bronze statues. We turned down a darkened hallway, and then suddenly we stepped out into an area that was brightly lit. Our procession formed four columns, came to a halt, and made a right face. I just stood there blinking and slowly realized that I was standing on the stage of the Paris Opera House, the *palais Opéra Garnier!* Facing us was an audience in formal attire, enthusiastically applauding. Scattered among them were a few American and British military officers. A conductor stepped out from the wings, turned to face us, and lifted his baton. The 133rd Field Artillery Chorus was going to sing. And there I was, standing in the fourth row, an old Texas cowboy who couldn't sing a note.

"This meal was going to be a lot more expensive than I had anticipated. I decided my only option was to watch the conductor, move my mouth, and pray. *Lord, I have marched the length of France through ice and mud, spent a long bitter winter under big guns day and night with no relief for weeks on end. I have dodged mortar fire until it has become commonplace, and even gone without food for days at a time. I know the war will end soon, and I'm going to live to go home, if you'll just get me through this one.*

"I opened my mouth and silently pretended to sing along with the choir. I knew if I made a single sound, that French conductor would know the truth.

"I thought it was going pretty well until, right in the middle of a pause between songs, a voice from the audience blurted, 'Oh mah *Gawd,* there's ole Richard!' I recognized the voice of an old boy I'd known back at Camp Bowie. I felt my face burning and wondered if the whole audience knew that I was 'Ole Richard,' the impostor."

That's where my father, "Ole Richard," always ended the story. I don't think we ever heard how it all turned out for him. He seemed to enjoy the joke on himself, so I guess he got away with that escapade.

I don't think *anyone* in his Scottish family could sing. But while their upbringing may have been lacking in the arts, life on their West Texas ranch did give them many skills, a strong work ethic, and a fun-loving sense of adventure.

My father's brothers and sisters all left the ranch to pursue various occupations, but they could still work cattle. They came home to demonstrate their skill whenever Grandmother needed them. While they worked, the two younger boys teased Uncle John and my dad, the two eldest, about being "stove-up ole has-beens." They, in turn, grumbled good-naturedly about having to work with "a pair of ornery greenhorns." The four never stopped competing, and they had a knack for making even the dirtiest work seem like a game. For a few days back there on the ranch, they felt like kids again. Grandmother always said they were "a *famous batch,* and good hands all." She was proud that her boys were good with animals, just as their father had been.

Once when they were moving heifers from one pasture to another, I watched from a distance. Their faces were streaked with red dirt and sweat, but it was obvious they were having fun. My dad, on the big dappled gray, wore a wide grin. I could hear my uncles whooping to urge the cattle along. Uncle Roy reined up near the gate, and just as the first of the heifers started through, I heard Dad call out, "Sweet ladies down the middle. Now promenade all!"

It was hard to imagine those heifers as "ladies," and they weren't promenading very gracefully, but I guess he saw herding cattle like calling square dances.

From time to time someone mentioned that Uncle John and Dad were good at "talking livestock down," whatever that meant. They made it sound like they could take a frightened animal and just about *hypnotize* him. Once my Aunt Nan said, "Richard *sings to them* just like our papa did, just the way cowhands have always done, I guess." I said, "Aunt Nan, my daddy can't sing, at least not anything but square dance calls." His vocal range was certainly limited, but I guess the animals didn't care. They must have appreciated his odd chanting, because every now and then that "singing" ability came in handy.

Now, the *song* may have been unimportant. It was probably my father's careful observation and understanding of the animal's behavior, along with his quiet approach, that lulled them into submission.

The first time I heard the strange rhythmic chant he used, he was calming a feisty young bull. I was still quite small then, and since I didn't recognize any of the words, I thought it was just gobbledygook. A couple of years later, I heard him sing that same unintelligible chant in another situation, and this time I was more impressed.

One of our neighbors had a big, ill-tempered dog named Brutus. That mean old dog chased cars, and one afternoon, right in front of our house, a car hit him. Frightened and wild with pain, Brutus began to snarl and snap, keeping all potential rescuers at bay. A cluster of curious spectators gathered, and by the time we came on the scene, Brutus had already chomped down on one helpful neighbor and had even bitten his master! Now, Brutus was locked in an awkward, menacing posture. There was a gash on his left flank, and the leg dangled. Dad surveyed the situation and said, "Let's see if I can just ease up on him."

The onlookers moved back and fell silent. Dad took one step out of the group and stood very still. Then he began that soft, rhythmic chant that my brother called "mumbo-jumbo." I only remember a few of the sounds, "Ai Gude keep's aa nae hairm . . . nae dylt . . ." He moved slowly forward, just a few inches at a time. He continued the quiet, monotonous chanting, "a glender-gane tae daith . . ." I watched, almost afraid to breathe. But after a little while I decided that my dad's "gobbledygook" must be some sort of magic incantation, because that huge, terrified dog gradually stopped his growling. ". . . nae diel . . . nae fant." Brutus held the same unnatural stance, but he wasn't snarling anymore. Head lowered, he returned Dad's steady gaze for what seemed like a long time. Still chanting the repetitious verse, Dad finally moved in close enough to put out his hand and stroke Brutus gently along his back. "Aa doutance, mait . . . easedom . . . guid . . . nae effere." He slipped a short loop of rope around the dog's muzzle. Brutus tried to sit, but couldn't. He whimpered, but let Dad lift him gently while my brother slid an improvised stretcher underneath him. Dad kept chanting in a slow steady cadence, "Gweed yym . . . nae efferre . . ." He continued to stroke Brutus until they had lifted him safely into the bed of a pickup beside his owner. I decided my dad had supernatural powers.

On our next visit to Grandmother's house, I couldn't wait to tell her how *my dad* was the hero who had calmed the vicious dog with his magic chant. She just nodded in her usual matter-of-fact way and said, "His father taught him how to use that song." Well, that ended my boast, and I felt so deflated that I didn't ask, "What song, Grandmother? Tell me about the song."

I had reached my teens before I heard the chant again, when my older brother and sister began to bring their young families home to visit. We all enjoyed the babies. Dad could always make them laugh, but my mother cautioned, "Don't ever give Grandpa Dick a fussy baby unless you're really ready for him to go to sleep. He puts babies to sleep."

It was true. Often when a baby was cutting teeth, had colic, or was just wailing to be fed, Dad would say, "Why don't you let me have that baby?" My sister or sister-in-law usually handed over the little screamer and then headed for the kitchen to warm a bottle. She would return only minutes later to find the baby sleeping peacefully in his grandfather's arms. Dad was always sitting there, patting his foot, and softly chanting that same strange chant. ". . . gude keep's aa nae hairm . . . nae effere . . ." By then we had all gotten used to that song. It was just something our father did.

Although Dad could make a game of working cattle, the chant wasn't play to him. He used it to accomplish its soothing purpose only when he felt it was needed. It was serious business, and although he couldn't sing, the animals and babies didn't mind his three-note range, and they didn't even care that once he had been the only silent member of a choir that sang in the Paris Opera House. They understood his chant.

I can't recall the words of that singsong verse, and by the time I thought to ask about it, all those in my father's family who could have told me its origin were gone. Perhaps the words were only nonsense. But now I know that some of those sounds are reminiscent of Gaelic. No one had ever explained to me that long ago my Scottish ancestors had used another language, but Grandmother had said my dad learned the "song" from his father. . . . Had my grandfather improvised that verse to calm a skittish colt or some restless bull? Perhaps that chant went so far back in the family's history that no one knew where it began. If the grandfather that I never knew, or my father, had actually known any Gaelic words, no one had ever mentioned it. Maybe both of them had sung the ancient words without ever knowing what they meant. I suspect the song may have been a Gaelic form of what our American trail-riding cowboys called "a night song," sung to keep the cattle calm.

I'm haunted by the thought that the song may have passed from father to son through generations of our Scottish family and now is lost. I'm left with only the memory of the chant's compelling rhythm, its calming effect, and so many questions that will never be answered.

Though I'll always remember the chant my dad sang to animals and babies as being serious business, there was another number he sang just for fun. Often when he puttered in his workshop or did repairs around the house, I heard this square dance call:

Up the river and around the bend,
Grab your gal and we're gone again.
The Fort Worth Record and the Dallas News,
Now swing that gal in the high-topped shoes!

It made me want to take his arm and swing all the way to Paris.

Richard the Spy

My father, Richard, was an honest country boy. He came straight off a West Texas ranch. He stood six feet four inches in his stocking feet, had an enormous shock of dark red hair, a face full of freckles, rough Scottish features, and an easy grin. On his feet were size 13½ AAAA boots. Old Richard's athletic ability helped get him started in the business world, and his keen sense of humor contributed to his success. In time he was at home in cities far and wide, but there was always just a touch of the country about him. It was his love for the newly popular game of football that took him away to the university.

When he came back to the little West Texas town he looked different. He had changed his boots and ranch wear for well-polished shoes, custom-tailored shirts, and suits with sleeves that were actually long enough. And he had a new title: attorney-at-law. He was ready to settle down to a law practice, but there was a war brewing in Europe. It was called the Great War, the "war to end all wars." Old Richard, country boy and patriot, volunteered. When he finally came home again he was older and more solemn, and there were parts of three fingers missing from his right hand.

He went to work in the legal office of a big farm machinery company's exports division, and in time he became what used to be known as a *company man*. He did well. He married tiny Eula and together they raised a houseful of children, including four boys who weren't even theirs. They had a pleasant life.

He often traveled for the company, and a little ritual emerged. He would come home and say, "Eula, will you help me pack?" And together they would get out his handsome Gladstone suitcase and pack clothes for some different climate, a small Bible, and a little leather folder with pictures of Eula and each of the children. As the packing or unpacking progressed, the children came to sit on the floor in their parents' bedroom. Each would check to see that *his* picture was in place in the little folder. And they listened because as he packed, Richard told them stories of places he had been and people he had met, or where he was going now.

The family always went to the railway station to stand on the platform and wave good-bye. They thought he was very handsome and very impressive, standing there in the vestibule of the railway car in his tailored suit with his leather bag and briefcase. For Richard and his family, life was good.

But another war was brewing. It was World War II, and this time old Richard's boys were all just the right age to go. Old Richard raised a victory garden that covered half a city block. A country boy could do that to help the war effort. To save tires and gasoline, he tied his briefcase to the handlebars of an old bicycle, and in his tailored suits he pedaled to work.

Now, it was a time when everyone was cautioned about talking to strangers. We were told not to discuss war-related jobs or talk about where our servicemen were around people we didn't know. Posters everywhere cautioned that "A Careless Lip Can Sink a Ship" and to beware of something called the "fifth column." Everyone was reminded not to buy on the "black market." It was a time of shortages, as the nation's industries made the war effort their priority. There were shortages of everything made of metal, rubber, or leather, and rationing was begun on things like sugar, shoes, meat, tires, gasoline, and farm machinery.

The farm machinery company's manufacturing plants were retooled to make weapons, tanks, and troop trucks. And they needed a man they could trust to allocate the few farm implements they had to places that were most essential to meeting the nation's needs. They looked for someone who knew farming and ranching, a loyal company man. They found Richard. He took the responsibility seriously and worked long hours making sure that machinery went to the proper places. Gradually, however, he became aware that some of the implements were finding their way into the black market. That worried him.

One day in the middle of the war, he came home and asked Eula to help him pack for a trip to Chicago. There was nothing unusual about that. But the way he came home from that trip was strange. He hadn't come by train. He had arrived in a 1937 Plymouth coupe, all rust and rattles and caked with mud.

In addition to his usual leather bag he brought with him an old striped cardboard suitcase filled with worn khaki shirts and pants, and an old plaid mackinaw jacket with frayed cuffs and elbows. From the back of a closet he brought out his gardening shoes and a tired felt hat with a greasy band. He packed the little Bible and the leather folder with the photographs in the cardboard suitcase. As he packed, he said quietly to Eula, "I'll be gone for quite a while. You probably won't hear from me. If there's an emergency . . ." Her heart nearly stopped. She knew he meant one of those dreaded telegrams the War Department sent when a serviceman was lost. She knew he was thinking of their boys. "If there's an emergency," he went on, "call this number in Chicago. Someone there will know how to find me. . . . No, I don't know how long this trip will take, but I'm sure you'll manage well without me."

She wasn't really frightened until she saw him place on the dresser a worn billfold that literally bulged with money. There were bills in large denominations and fat packets of extra gasoline ration stamps that they had never been entitled to use. She saw false identification cards from a gin and co-op over in Stonewall County, and even a draft registration card, and a driver's license. All bore the same strange name: Aaron Sanders. Now she was really terrified. She told herself that Richard was an honest and loyal company man, but it didn't calm her fears. He offered no word of explanation. He put on the ill-fitting khakis, topped by the mackinaw, got in that battered coupe, and drove away.

Weeks passed. Often family members wondered where he was and what he was doing, but they tried not to talk about their concerns. When they wrote letters to their boys overseas, they didn't mention his absence. Only once in all those weeks did they hear from him. On their wedding anniversary, Eula got a picture postcard of the Grand Canyon. It said simply, "Thinking of you, Aaron." She read the card and frowned, and then she shook her head and began to laugh, "I don't know what to make of that." She tucked the card away in the back of a drawer, out of sight.

Eventually he came home, without the coupe. He did bring with him a large mysterious box of papers, and for weeks he worked on them far into the night. Then he filed them away in a locked cabinet in the basement instead of taking them to the office. And he never talked about the trip. When one child asked questions, he said simply, "Someday we'll talk about that."

He didn't travel anymore after that, until finally the war ended, and the nation's servicemen began to come home. Trains and buses were all overcrowded. Travel was very difficult. One day Richard came home and asked, "Eula, will you help me pack?" She looked apprehensive and waited to see what clothes he packed. To her relief, he began to pack tailored shirts and suits. Since I was the only child young enough to still be at home, I sat on the floor and checked to see that the photographs were all in place in the leather folder. At long last, while my father packed, he began to tell me the story of the long, mysterious trip.

He said it had been a trip of great importance, and it had been a grand adventure. It seems that wherever he stopped, he registered in a second-class hotel under the name of *Aaron Sanders*. Then he stood around on a street corner where men gathered to spit and whittle. He whittled a little, and listened a lot, quietly letting it be known that he was in the market for some farm machinery, and he could pay cash. In some towns he bought implements, and in others he couldn't. He told delightedly of one town where the implement dealer not only told him he didn't sell on the black market, but he picked up a baseball bat and chased him out of his store. Richard loved that. But sometimes, in other towns, he bought from dealers who were all too willing to be black marketeers for a price. In one place he bought a tractor, in another a disk-harrow, and in still another, a combine. He paid cash but carefully obtained receipts with signatures. Sales were invoiced, and each implement was shipped to a rural address, which was, in fact, a warehouse not far from Abilene. There, every piece was tagged and stored to wait.

He told funny stories, too. He said his first week didn't go very well. The first night he was preparing to sign his newly assumed name to a hotel registry when a voice behind him exclaimed, "Well, if it isn't old Richard!" He turned around to see an old World War I buddy who looked him up and down in the worn khakis and the mackinaw with frayed sleeves, and said, "It looks to me like the promising young lawyer hasn't done any better than the rest of us." Richard muttered something about having "a little trouble with the law," signed his own name to the registry, and left town the next morning.

Later that same week he was in the city of El Paso when the Plymouth coupe began to sputter. Richard was using the choke to keep it from stalling, watching afternoon traffic, and looking for highway markers. In the middle of all that, he encountered the first intersection he had ever seen in the new design called a "cloverleaf." Somehow—between the faltering car, the traffic, and the signs—he got into a loop of that cloverleaf headed the wrong direction.

Almost immediately he heard a siren and saw a police car in his rearview mirror. He pulled as near to the curb as possible and reached into his pocket for his yet untried driver's license showing his new name. He said he was thinking, "It would happen to me *here*, on an international border, in the middle of the war. I'm going to hand false identification papers to a law enforcement officer." Richard said that for a moment he saw his legal career in serious jeopardy.

A tired old officer walked forward, examining the battered coupe. He said, "What's the matter, fella, can't you *read?*" Richard, always a good deadpan liar, said, "Yes, sir. I can read *printin'*." The officer stepped back to see the car door open, and Richard beginning to disentangle his long legs from under the steering wheel. As he emerged and unfolded to his full height, the officer looked this man over. Richard stood solemnly in the khakis, with his boney wrists dangling out of the mackinaw sleeves. He clutched his hat in front of him, and in his best country voice, said, "Good afternoon, officer. I sure hope I haven't done anything wrong."

The officer shook his head, "Where in the hell are you from?" Old Richard announced, "I'm from Old Glo-ry." Now, the officer didn't know where Stonewall County was, and he had never heard of Old Glory, but he figured he had a real hayseed on his hands. With exaggerated patience, he explained the layout of the cloverleaf intersection. The explanation finished, Richard said, "Thank you, officer, and I hope I haven't caused any trouble." Out of the corner of his eye, he was amused to see that traffic was backed up around the curve and out of sight. Beginning to enjoy his dramatic role, and still in character, he added, "I'd sure be much obliged to you, sir, if you could stop those cars while I turn around and get headed in the right direction." The long-suffering officer stopped the traffic to let him turn the stalling, sputtering car around. Then as an afterthought, he said, "Maybe I'd better lead you through the loop and out to your highway." Once he was out on the highway, Richard put his long skinny foot to the accelerator, and headed off toward Carlsbad, laughing all the way.

Richard was still grinning at the memory when he finished packing the Gladstone bag and brought his stories to an end. He brought the mysterious papers from the locked filing cabinet and loaded them into a green metal box with a lock and a handle. He had somehow managed to get a Pullman compartment with room enough to accommodate him and the metal box at a time when even a Pullman berth was almost unobtainable. Eula said, "Aren't you going to check that thing as baggage?" His reply was, "No, I'd like to keep my eye on it." At the railway station he handed his suitcase to the porter but carried the heavy green box up the steps of the Pullman car himself and turned to wave good-bye to his family. He was off to Chicago.

Now, about that same time, a scattered group of farm machinery dealers opened important-looking letters requesting their presence at a meeting in the implement company's Chicago office. Their prepaid travel had already been arranged.

The dealers arrived in Chicago, considering themselves part of a select group of some kind. They talked among themselves: "This meeting probably concerns post-war expansion plans." Were new equipment designs to be unveiled? Why had they been chosen for the meeting? As they convened, however, the atmosphere seemed more like a legal hearing, presided over by a company vice president and a tall, rawboned company attorney who wore a well-tailored suit but had just a bit of a country air about him. Some dealers thought he looked familiar. Others noticed that parts of three fingers were missing from the attorney's right hand. That may have stirred a distant memory for one or two.

In an individual session with each dealer, that same man carefully documented their illegal sales and then explained to each that their dealership arrangement with the implement company was terminated with the end of business on that same day. Some denied even their own signatures and receipts on their dealership's printed forms. Some said they had never seen this man before and couldn't possibly have made the sale in question. One or two said he did look familiar. They thought they remembered a handshake from just such a hand. One admitted everything, saying he "remembered that old guy, because he had the longest, skinniest feet I ever saw." But old Richard, the spy, offered no ready grin or easy humor that day. He was still an honest country boy, a patriotic lawyer, and a loyal company man.

A Company Christmas

In 1831 Cyrus Hall McCormick invented the reaper, and the farm machinery company that began with that event was to become an international firm, with manufacturing plants, distribution branches, and dealerships across the United States and abroad. Long before I was born, my father had begun a lifelong career with that concern—International Harvester. The history of our lives was connected to The Company.

The local branch house had the biggest payroll in our little town. When 1929's stock-market crash caused payroll cutbacks, "the company" told its career employees it would keep them on until the bad times ended, if they would cover the jobs the company needed them to do. In some cases that meant people transferred to a branch in another state; sometimes it meant quite a reduction in pay. But it guaranteed a regular income and the company's promise of employment.

In any small town the IHC management team's regular paychecks were envied by many self-employed heads of households who struggled to make ends meet. Our dad's friend Bill owned a custom cabinet shop. Mack, a local grocer, called Bill one day and asked him to build new fixtures for his store. He couldn't pay in cash, he said, but he'd cover the cost of the work in groceries. Bill said later that on the first day he got paid, when he got in his pickup and looked over his shoulder at all those groceries, he'd never felt so rich.

Our company thought of some interesting ways to take care of its families, maintain their loyalty, and at the same time let the community know how important the company's presence was to the local economy. One month the branch house paid its employees in silver dollars and asked them not to deposit them in a bank account as they would normally do with their paychecks, but instead to use them for all their expenses. When my mother paid for her groceries, the drawer of Mr. Pace's manual cash register made a loud *thud* as it flew open with the weight of all the silver dollars it held. When my dad counted out payment for some home repair materials at the local lumberyard, the man at the counter said, "I know who *you* work for!" Those silver dollars clanked into the collection plates of all the churches in town, and we paid our mortgage in eleven coins that month. At the end of many days the local department store manager lugged his daily receipts to the bank in heavy bags, thinking about IHC employees. Those silver dollars circulated around town for quite awhile.

That was the whole idea, of course. Not until many years later, when I began to study public relations, did I really comprehend the brilliance of that simple directive.

The year 1931 marked the one hundredth anniversary of the invention of the reaper—International Harvester's centennial year—and the company had bronze commemorative medals made. The medallions were about the size of a silver dollar but heavier, big enough to stand out in your pocket, anyway. On one side the early reaper was depicted, mounted in a kind of metal framework that it took two men to move along the rows—one up ahead riding the dray horse, and one walking behind to clear up the shocks of grain. On the other side of the bronze medal was a likeness of Cyrus McCormick, his strong jaw softened by a handsome beard. These were given to employees, dealers, and customers who bought farm machinery and trucks. When the company's centennial year was over, there were ten or twelve surplus medals at our house. Two or three of them I called mine, and at age four I dressed every morning in my corduroy overalls and put into my pockets two McCormick medals, two pennies, and a Dallas bus token. Without them, I just wasn't properly dressed.

When you walked upstairs from the showroom floor to the front offices at the International Harvester branch house, you could stop on the landing and look at two huge bronze replicas of both sides of those medals, heads and tails, eighteen inches across and mounted on a walnut board four feet long and a little better than two feet wide. If I stretched as high as I could, I just barely touched the bottom of that board. I often gazed at those big medallions and *wished* I could take them home. I thought, "*Those* are the ones I want."

I had to wait nearly forty years to own a set of those large medallions. They now hang in the foyer at my house. Every time I pass I smile at Cyrus Hall McCormick and think of the company that resulted from his genius. That company was such an integral part of my formative years.

At least once a year, the head of that company left his office, changed into his khakis and a hard hat, and traveled around to every IHC manufacturing plant. He walked every one of the company's assembly lines, listening to suggestions from just about everybody, with someone at his elbow taking notes. From place to place, he addressed longtime employees by name, asked about work or family, and shook the hands of newer employees.

Occasionally the head of that company, a descendant of old Cyrus McCormick, came to Texas to hunt with the local branch manager and my dad. Once or twice he came to our house for dinner. He acted like family, but my mother cooked like she was feeding royalty. IHC was a company that had never known a labor strike, a company with a reputation for taking care of its people.

Now, when I was a small child, some of my friends argued about how Santa Claus got into houses without chimneys because in West

Texas we didn't have a lot of chimneys. Some said he could come through a front door even if it was locked, and some said he came in through a window. Of course, lots of children didn't expect Santa Claus at all during the Depression, and maybe they comforted themselves thinking it was the lack of a chimney that was to blame. We all pretty much agreed that the store Santas weren't real. We called them Santa's "helpers." How *could* they be real, with that dirty imitation fur on the cuffs of their red suits?

I knew the *real* Santa Claus. He always made an appearance at the company Christmas party. No, he didn't come with reindeer. I knew that the real Santa Claus drove a tractor—a small, bright red Farmall pulling a sled loaded with drawstring bags full of toys. I knew he was real because he called each one of us by name—"Hello, little Henry, . . . Martha. Hey, Merry Christmas, Janie Fay!"—and he brought each one of us the toy of our dreams, even the ones we hadn't dared ask for in a letter. He brought dolls with organdy dresses to some of the girls; he brought Louis a chemistry set; and he brought me a whole china tea set with a tablecloth and tiny little napkins with blue trim that matched the design on the cups and saucers. How had he *known?!*

He was the real thing, all right. My Santa wore a suit made of deep cherry-red velvet, trimmed with real white rabbit fur cuffs and collar. His beard and hair were long and curly white, just like the one drinking Coca-Cola on the calendar at the filling station. And he wore tiny gold-rimmed spectacles on his nose.

At International Harvester, the Christmas season began just a few days before Thanksgiving. My mother and I would go down to pick up my dad after work, and the men would be unloading what was surely the biggest Christmas tree in the world. Tied to the truck, it stretched the whole length of the flatbed and even hung off the end some. Within a few hours, the tree would be standing tall and glorious in the showroom window, surrounded by women standing on stepladders and stringing up lights. People who came to look would stand amazed, gazing from trunk to treetop, guessing its height.

During December the town's entertainment consisted of walking around the square, taking in the decorated store windows, and going to various Christmas music programs at the churches and schools. Every church had a Christmas pageant in which adolescent boys in false beards, turbans, and bathrobes reverently carried their gifts of big perfume bottles and powder boxes to the Christ child.

That month, Santa's elves, the International Harvester secretaries, divvied up a very long list and went shopping until they found just the right gift for each employee's child. About a week before the big day, the branch had a Christmas dinner for all 150 employees and their families. We went dressed up in our Sunday duds—you couldn't go to meet Santa Claus in your play clothes! *Everybody* was there, from the branch manager and his wife and son to the families of the two porters, Jack and Gilberto. There was turkey, of course, and ham, and all the Christmas trimmings you could imagine. We ate at long tables that filled the showroom, and then after dinner the men took down some of the tables and people would start to gather around the tree. The big, wide entrance from the warehouse, usually closed, was opened wide, and in Santa would ride on his bright red Farmall, waving and greeting everyone by name. At that point the women from the office upstairs would put on their elf caps. One by one they would pick up a package from under the tree and hand it to Santa Claus. He would call out the name on the gift and hand it to one of the children, along with a stocking filled with fruit and nuts and candy. Each child knew he would get a wonderful present. The excitement of waiting for Santa to call your name was almost too much for some of us. The grown-ups would have us sit down along the floor near the tree, and you had to listen for Santa's booming voice to announce, "Ho, ho, yes, and Jo Beth's been a pretty good girl all year. I have a package here for you . . ." If the package was on the large side, our parents would jump up to help. It was a Christmas party to fill your heart and linger in your memory for a lifetime.

We were proud to be a part of the Harvester family. When the company had opened its distribution branch in our town, my dad said he was the first one to walk through the door, and he was the last one out when it closed. So we grieved when the company as we knew it was no more. Those of us who were part of that era now watch the news about strikes, scandals, and crimes that take place within the walls of large corporations and wonder what in the world happened.

Several years ago I threw a Christmas party for my university department's faculty and students, just as I did every year. One of my students, Lee Ann Grainger, came from a wealthy ranching family. As she came through the front foyer she exclaimed, "Where did you *get* those?!" She was looking at the giant McCormick medals mounted on the wall. She said, "We have a little one like that. Daddy turned it up in a field when he was plowing one day, and he was so excited when he brought it home to show us. I've always wondered who lost it on our place. It was a treasured artifact at our house. I've never seen another one like it. I didn't know there were any as big as these!" Lee Ann stood and stared at those medallions for the longest time. At last she said, "I can't wait to get home and tell my dad!" At that moment, I looked up at the big ones and just wished I still had those little bronze medals I used to carry in my pockets when I was four. I thought, "*Those* are the ones I *really* want."

In generations past, the owner of a brand new Farmall tractor may have felt his lucky McCormick medal drop out of his pocket as he walked back to the house one evening. And after that, he probably never felt completely dressed.

The Boy

THE KITCHEN WAS WARM AND DINNER SMELLED GREAT, BUT from the window, it looked like the whole world was covered with ice. Sleet was hitting the kitchen windows hard. I could see Charlie and Jimmy covering the last of Mother's rosebushes. They began to scrape ice from the back steps, laughing as Rob went slipping and sliding around the corner toward the side porch with his shovel. Today I was glad I was a girl. At least my big sister and I had chores indoors.

It was mid-Depression, and I was only five, so I didn't know much about cooking, but I did know my jobs. Everybody had chores to do. I set the table and pulled chairs into place. One at each end for Mother and Daddy, two on the side nearest the kitchen for Jeannie and me, and since Jimmy and Rob had come to live with us, there were chairs across from us for the three teenaged boys. I was ready to fill glasses and help bring the food, but Daddy hadn't come home yet from work.

Mother looked at the big kitchen clock and frowned. I'm sure she wondered if he was having trouble driving home on the icy streets. Charlie and Rob came in together and left their coats and boots in the back hall. Rob came into the kitchen, sneaked up behind Jeannie, and tried to put his cold fingers on the back of her neck. She squealed, "Oh, get away from me! You're freezing!"

Mother wanted to know, "Where's Jimmy? Did you leave him out on the ice?" "Oh, he's as bad as Rosy about animals," Rob complained. "He brought that old stray cat into the workshop, and he's making a bed for it in a box."

When Jimmy came in, the boys headed upstairs to wash up for dinner, and Charlie called from the landing, "Dad's car just turned into the driveway, Mom. Looks like he has someone with him." Mother frowned, probably thinking that it wasn't only the children who brought home strays.

We heard the side door open and close, and then there were shuffling steps in the hall. We waited for Daddy to open the kitchen door with his usual grin and humorous greeting for Mom and Jeannie. He always turned to me last and said, "Hello there, Funnyface." But this time he opened the kitchen door just a crack and said, "Eula, could I see you out here for a minute?" We all looked surprised, and Mother headed for the hall. Charlie came down the stairs and into the kitchen. "What's going on? There's someone in the downstairs bathroom. I just got a glimpse of him in the hallway. It looked like a kid, all wrapped up in that old army blanket Daddy keeps in the car." The other boys joined us. We heard the sound of water running, and Rob said, "They're filling the bathtub!"

Mother came back to the kitchen, and as she turned down the burners on the stove, she began to give orders. "Dinner will have to wait. Jean, don't dish anything up yet. Just keep it warm and don't let anything burn. Rosy, you set another place at the table. Rob, there's a pair of barber scissors on my dresser. Please get them for me." She paused, and her face looked so solemn that we knew she was concentrating on something important. She continued, "And two or three big grocery bags too, please." She turned to Charlie next, "You go upstairs and find a set of your underwear, some socks, khaki pants, and a shirt. Bring the smallest ones you can find." To Jimmy she said, "Do you know where we put those clothes for the mission? They're in the storeroom. Bring me the smallest pair of boy's shoes, and a big bar of lye soap."

We looked at each other curiously and then scattered in all directions. If there was one thing this family knew how to do, it was to obey orders in an emergency. Mother added, "Rosy, get that big jar of soup out of the refrigerator, so Jean can heat it up." I wanted to ask why, but I didn't. Jean looked at me and shrugged. Soon we heard Mother dialing the telephone in the hall. Rob came back and said, "She's calling the doctor." We tried to hear. She was saying, "Amos, don't laugh. Yes, I said *head lice.*" We heard her knock on the bathroom door and say, "Dick, he wants to talk to you." Daddy took the phone, and we heard him say, "I don't really know, Amos . . . thirteen or fourteen . . . no, no, I don't think there's any real frostbite . . . Yes, I know how to do that. We'll see you later then." And he hung up the phone. Mother came back, poured hot soup into a big cup, and went out again. We waited. All we knew was that our Dad had brought a boy home with him, and apparently he was sick, or hurt . . . and he had lice!

On Mother's next trip through the kitchen, she looked at our puzzled faces and stopped long enough to explain, "Well, it's a boy, and he's not in good shape." Daddy called out, "Charlie, put on your coat and come take some things out to the trash barrel." Next we heard him say, "See if you can get all of this to burn. I know it's wet and icy, but try. Here, don't get any of these things up against you." Charlie went out the back door with two grocery bags crammed with what appeared to be clothing. He was holding the bags at arm's length. Mother sent Jimmy upstairs to put sheets and covers on the extra bed.

When she finally said we could put food on the table, we were ready to get a look at this boy. She said, "Charlie, you sit over here by Rosy this time, and leave that place next to Daddy for the boy." We stood behind our chairs. Daddy was talking quietly to the stranger as they came in. He wasn't very tall, and in the oversized clothes he looked very thin. He kept his head down and looked up at us with large, frightened eyes. His blonde hair had obviously just been cut off close to his head, and there were red welts on his scalp. He smelled like lye soap and sulfur. We could see a large, partially healed bruise along his cheek. Daddy helped him pull out a chair, and as he sat down, his eyes were fixed on the platter of roast beef in front of him. He stuck out his hand toward it, but Daddy gently touched the boy's arm and said, "Son, we bow our heads and offer a prayer of thanks before we eat." The boy jerked back and looked up at Daddy as though he wasn't quite sure what that meant. We bowed our heads, and Daddy's deep voice began. The prayer seemed different this time. He spoke of safety and shelter, then food. I couldn't stand it. I opened my eyes and peeked at the strange boy. Wide-eyed, he was staring around the table, then at me. I tucked my head, embarrassed to have been caught. As the prayer ended, Jimmy leaned toward him and said, "It's all right. Rob and I had never done that either until we came here to live last year." The boy shot him a glance of complete puzzlement.

Daddy was saying, "Now, this is our family. You met Mother. This is Jean, and Rosy and Charlie. Jim is next to you there, and that's Rob on the end." Charlie asked, "What's your name?" The boy ducked and shook his head. Daddy reassured him, "It's all right. That can wait. Now, you can have all you want to eat, but remember what I told you. You need to eat very slowly or you'll be sick."

Daddy helped him with the serving dishes. The boy's hands trembled, and as we all began to eat, we tried not to notice how he stuffed the food into his mouth. Daddy kept reminding him to eat slowly.

When dinner finally ended, Rob led the way toward the hall door. Daddy said, "We'll get you settled upstairs now." They passed the corner of the table where there was one biscuit left on the bread plate. The boy's hand shot out, and in a flash the biscuit disappeared into his pants pocket. Jeannie and I both saw it. Jeannie started to say something, but Dad shook his head silently, and we kept quiet.

They continued up the stairs, and we heard the boy speak for the first time. He looked up at our dad and said, "Are you a preacher-man?" Daddy chuckled, "No son, I'm just the dad in this house."

Jeannie and I went about the business of clearing away the dishes. When Uncle Doc arrived, he came all the way back to the kitchen before he put down his bag, took off his gloves, and began to warm his hands. He wrinkled his nose at me and said, "Well, little worry-wart, at least you're not the one who needs me this time." Then he turned to Mother. "Well, let's go upstairs and have a look at what Dick has brought home this time." Mother just smiled and went with him. She didn't have to explain much to Uncle Doc.

It was several days before the boy was well enough to be out of bed for more than a few minutes at a time. Sometimes we heard him crying out in his sleep, and one of the boys would sit by him until he was calm again. Rob told us there were scars on his back and shoulders. A big ugly burn on his back was infected. Uncle Doc or Daddy put a fresh dressing on it every day. It was obvious the strange boy had been badly treated, but we knew little else about him. It was almost two weeks before he told us that his name was Don.

When he did finally start talking, we couldn't stop him. He had a thousand questions: What town was this? Were we in Oklahoma or Texas? How did Jeannie learn to play the piano like that? Where did Charlie and Jimmy get those red band uniforms? Why did we have so many musical instruments around here? What did the boys mean when they said they were Boy Scouts? We discovered he had never been to school for very long at a time, and that he had never in his life been inside a church.

As the weeks passed, Daddy said Don had to go to school, but he had no birth certificate, no grade report, and no vaccination record. Daddy arranged some kind of guardianship, and Uncle Doc took care of the TB test and vaccinations. He was enrolled at Bowie Elementary School in Mrs. Clark's sixth grade room, but he was taller and older than the other students there, which embarrassed him. Right away he was determined to catch up, so he could be in the eighth grade with Rob in junior high.

The whole family pitched in to tutor Don. Rob and Jimmy taught him to ride their old dilapidated bicycles and how to patch inner tubes and fix flats in the worn tires. Jeannie began to teach him a few of the songs she played. At our lake cabin he learned to fish and manage a rowboat. He roasted wieners and toasted marshmallows. Charlie gave him swimming lessons. We learned that he had a natural talent for baseball. Most of all, Don was learning to be part of a family.

NEARLY THIRTY YEARS LATER, Uncle Doc and Dad were puzzling over their Saturday afternoon chess game, and out of the silence Uncle Doc said, "You know, Dick, back during the Depression I was always amazed that, with three children of your own, you and Eula actually managed to take in those extra boys. How on earth did you *do* that?"

Dad said, "Oh, it was pretty close sometimes, but we made it. And you were always there when we needed you." Still staring at the chessmen, he continued, "I think the best part about the whole thing is that they all turned out well. There wasn't a bad apple in the bunch." Uncle Doc shook his head. "Well, the one I had my doubts about was Don. Where did you get him, out of a boxcar?"

Dad grinned and nodded. "Something like that. I was leaving work that afternoon. Everything was icy, and the streets were nearly deserted. I looked down toward the railroad a block or two away, and I saw someone stumbling across the tracks on the ice. I just turned down that way, and as I drove along the switchyard, I could see he was just a boy. I stopped and called out, 'Young man, are you alone out here?' You know, he ran from me and tried to go up the embankment to the overpass. Of course, he slipped on the ice. As he came sliding down, I just put out my hand and caught him by the arm. I could see he was scared to death. I said, 'Son, we need to get you in where it's warm.' He was too weak to offer much resistance. I just wrapped him up in a blanket and brought him home."

Uncle Doc added, "I asked him once why he ran from you that day. He said he 'saw a tall man in a suit and hat get out of that big black car, and he thought it was the law.'" They both chuckled, and Uncle Doc continued, "I won't ever forget the first time I saw him. He sure was a mess." Dad grinned, "I thought he was looking pretty good by the time you got there. We had already cut his hair, burned his clothes, and given him a G.I. bath. You should have seen Eula's face when she first got a look at him and realized he had a head full of lice." They both laughed. Uncle Doc shook his head again, "He was a sick little boy, and he was a sorry sight." Then Daddy said, "Well I guess we'd better speak more respectfully of him now. After all, as of last month, he's Lieutenant Colonel Wilkins." They nodded together with a look of satisfaction. And the two old friends went quietly back to their chess game.

Balmorhea, Summer 1939

IN THE PHOTOGRAPH I AM NINE YEARS OLD, HOLDING THE TALL stalk of a century plant in each hand. My right hand grasps a fourteen-foot plant in full bloom; in my left I hold a leaning ten-footer. Bees swarm around the sticky, yellow-green flowers high overhead, blooms that appear only once in the plant's lifetime of about twenty years. The dry grass underfoot is sparse, the way it gets when there's no water and nothing to shield it from the West Texas sun.

We were on one of our "mystery trips" that day, one of many I took that summer in Balmorhea with my mother's younger sister, Gladys, my Uncle Thurman, and my grandmother, whom everybody called "Woodsie." We usually took along Huaco, too, my aunt and uncle's Mexican Hairless Sholo, a small brown dog devoid of hair except for a tuft on the top of his head that looked like a tiny auburn toupee.

A few months earlier I had overheard my parents having a serious conversation about Gladys, who was only twenty-eight years old. She was sick with something they called "leukemia." Woodsie wanted to take care of Gladys and had decided to spend the summer in Balmorhea. She convinced my parents that I should go with her. Early one June morning, Woodsie and I set off on a Greyhound bus.

My aunt and uncle met us in Pecos. There I got my first look at the part of Texas where the legendary Judge Roy Bean had once proclaimed himself "the law west of the Pecos." In the distance stood the Davis Mountains. They said the silhouette of those mountains looked like a reclining lady with her hair flowing out behind her, but I never could see them that way, no matter how hard I looked.

My Uncle Thurman was a civil engineer, a graduate of Texas A&M. The U.S. Army Corps of Engineers had set up an office in the community of Balmorhea to make topographical maps of the Davis Mountains and the Big Bend (now Big Bend National Park), and my uncle was supervising the construction of some of the first improved roads through that part of far West Texas. The gravel road that went through the middle of Balmorhea couldn't have been called *improved.* It had an irrigation ditch running the length of it, straight down the center. Along that boulevard was a general store, and a drugstore that had been closed for months. There was a movie theater that opened on Saturday nights for the one showing of the weekly movie. The little union church had a maximum seating capacity of about twenty-five, and no one could remember ever seeing it filled to capacity. There were a few houses with tin roofs and a U.S. post office. That was about it.

Most of that summer, Aunt Gladys stayed in bed. Sometimes she was up and around, but sometimes she felt so bad that she cried. And because the focus was on her care, I had a lot of time to myself. So I made friends with the few children near my own age. Two sisters lived nearby, Yvonne and Charley Joyce (the latter named for her father), and a tall, quiet girl we all called "Birdy Mae" lived around the corner. The summer was over before I realized that her name was Berta Mae. When Yvonne's birthday was coming up, Aunt Gladys was feeling better, and Woodsie planned a party as a diversion.

The guests all had party hats made of the black-and-white daily comic strips from the Pecos newspaper, but the Birthday Girl's hat was made from the brightly colored Sunday funnies. For gifts we made clothes for Yvonne's doll. Gladys and I sewed her a pair of pajamas and a dress with a matching bonnet, and Woodsie crocheted her some booties and a tiny sweater. That started a flurry of doll wardrobe-making from the whole group of girls. We spent several hot summer days on our screened-in porch seriously stitching left-over scraps of fabric into miniature costumes. When we tired of dressing up our dolls, we dressed Yvonne and Charley Joyce's new litter of kittens in real calico. And finally, our interest in fashion turned to ourselves.

For weeks we played dress-up. I could hardly part with a pair of Aunt Gladys's high-heeled shoes and a frilly hat. Every day in the late afternoon I was sent to pick up our mail. I would wear my fashion all the way to the post office, clopping down the road with the hem of my dress dragging a trail in the dirt. By the time I got back home, I was tired of the high heels.

"Going for the mail" was the only regular social event in Balmorhea. People ambled in from all directions to stand around in front of the post office visiting with friends while waiting for the elderly postmaster to finish pushing the letters, newspapers, and an occasional package into the forty or so boxes on the wall. When he had finished, he always called out, "Mail's up!"

Everyone tried to squeeze into the tiny building at once, although they knew only three or four at a time could get near enough to the boxes to see if they had mail. A short line formed to ask about general delivery letters. My uncle said some people just couldn't pay to rent mailboxes because of the Depression. I always felt very grown up when I turned the key in the front of our box. Later I noticed that few residents locked their boxes. One old fellow told me, "It's just too much bother to keep up with that little ole key, and besides, if some fool wants the bills in my box, he is shore as shootin' welcome to 'em!" Perhaps others felt the same way when they pulled their boxes open and sighed as they checked the contents. I noticed there were a few, however, who looked in and even slid a hand inside to be sure no precious mail was overlooked. At those post office outings several people learned my name. Some inquired about my aunt's health or commented on my high-heeled finery. I was becoming part of the local color.

We spent many afternoons trying to float down the irrigation ditch that ran through town. The water was so shallow, and the bottom of the ditch so rocky, we tried to protect ourselves by riding in cardboard boxes or just sitting on sheets of cardboard until they were soaked. By mid-July, the seats of our bathing suits wore through and required mending, and before summer's end we gave up on the bathing suits and wore shirts and old cut-off trousers instead.

On special occasions we went swimming in the natural spring-fed pool on the edge of town. It was the only recreation spot in Balmorhea. Far below us in the deep water near the rocky edges enormous catfish swam past, twitching their long whiskers. We loved the icy cold water, but we didn't go to the pool very often because it cost a nickel to get in, and we didn't have many nickels.

Now and then when there was someone to conduct the service, we went to church, held up our *Glad Tidings* hymnals, and sang songs like

Are you warshed in the blood,
In the soul-cleansin' bloo-ood of the Lamb?
Are your garments spotless? Are they white as snow?
Are you warshed in the bloo-ood of the Lamb?

which I always thought made no sense at all. The ten or twelve of us would stretch out our necks and give it all we had, which meant that we raised a wealth of sound, most of which was nasal and off-key. It helped some when my Aunt Gladys felt well enough to be there and accompany us on the old, out-of-tune piano.

Uncle Thurman was an East Texan. One neighbor said "he was odd as a blue-eyed cow from away," but he adored my Aunt Gladys and devised "mystery trips" to entertain her on weekends when she felt well enough to go somewhere. She would beg him to tell her where he was taking us next, but he always kept it a secret, so we would be guessing all the way to our destination. We'd pack a picnic lunch of fried chicken, sandwiches, some fruit and cake, and a thermos of iced tea and head out in Uncle Thurman's Ford.

Once we went to see the Fort Davis ruins, one of the westernmost outposts in Texas, and Indian Lodge, a small vacation inn built of rustic stones and logs. Another time we went to the McDonald Observatory, where the domed ceiling opened up all by itself to reveal the sky. I couldn't believe that you could see faraway stars and planets through that huge telescope.

One day Aunt Gladys felt pretty good and put on her jodhpurs. She sat while Uncle Thurman helped her with her engineer's boots that laced up almost to the knee. We all got in the car, drove up into the mountains, and finally stopped near the top of a hill where there wasn't even a trail. We got out with our basket lunch and hiked a little farther up.

"Here it is!" said Uncle Thurman.

"Here is *what?* We don't see anything!" we said.

Then he pointed down, and there, on top of that hill where the soil had eroded, was a bed of pink rose quartz at least five or six feet in diameter! We dug down a few inches where the crystals were protected from the sun. There they were a deeper shade of pink, and Woodsie pulled out a nice-sized piece to take home for her garden. I put two pretty crystals in my pocket. What treasures! I often wished I knew the way back there, but I never remembered the routes we took on those trips to remote places.

On the mystery trip I remember most vividly, we drove far off the road, got out, and hiked up a slope to a big bluff. We looked down to see a lake fed by crystal clear spring water flowing from a rock crevice. Uncle Thurman said, "We call this Phantom Lake." I was sure that no other human being had ever seen this place, that we were strictly pioneers. And it may have been true, so untouched was the scene. He added, "I know a good place down here for a picnic." So we followed him, single file, down the slope through the knee-high grass, and along the edge of the water, so clear that the lake seemed only inches deep. My uncle held Huaco under one arm and carried the thermos jug with the other. Gladys walked behind him. Woodsie brought the picnic basket, and I followed, carrying the quilt.

Where the tall grass ended, we all stopped abruptly. Resting on its side in the shallow water beside us was a large animal skeleton, completely untouched. A mustang, Thurman said. The bones were bleached white, and a wide row of ribs curved up into the air. We fell silent and slowly walked past. I wanted to inspect it more closely, but Woodsie said, "No, come away. Don't disturb it." We rounded the curve of the lake, and a little farther along we spread out the quilt on the grass. My uncle led my aunt gently along the water's edge to show her how beautiful the glassy lake was in the sunlight with its clear, cold water flowing out of the spring somewhere deep in the crevice of the stone wall.

Woodsie and I spread out our picnic. When we all sat down to eat, I looked across the quilt at my Aunt Gladys. Her eyes were filled with tears, and my uncle kept his arm around her for a while.

On our walk back to the car, we made a wide arc around the mustang skeleton.

BY THAT YEAR my grandmother had already lost four of her eight children. One infant and a little boy died early. A daughter had died of a ruptured appendix on her fourteenth birthday. Another son, badly crippled with rheumatoid arthritis, had died of pneumonia at twenty-seven. Now, despite the fact that she was now spending her last days with Gladys, my amazing grandmother managed to remain surprisingly cheerful. As we bounced along down the hill that afternoon, she began to sing a funny song, and we all joined in as we always did. This time our quartet was a bit rowdier than usual.

The closest doctor was in Pecos, forty miles away. Every two weeks we drove there at thirty miles an hour, so he could see my aunt and check her blood count. We usually went on Saturday. The doctor's office was always open and busy because on Saturdays everybody went to town. We piled soft pillows into the front seat of the car for the long ride, and then Uncle Thurman would help Gladys in and prop her up to make her comfortable. Huaco always went along in back with Woodsie and me.

One Saturday evening on our way back to Balmorhea, we were headed west into the sunset. We counted the few cars we met, and we always waved. The land was flat, wide open, and mostly empty out that way, covered with miles and miles of green alfalfa. We came to a lone white farmhouse where there was usually a black pickup parked outside. Today the place looked deserted, and as we passed it Uncle Thurman suddenly called out, "Hey, look! There's a fox!" From a fence near the farmhouse, a flash of red fur darted across the highway. In the fox's mouth, hanging by its neck, was a chicken. Uncle honked the horn, and Huaco began to bark. The fox dropped the chicken, ran through the weeds of the shallow bar ditch, and began struggling under the barbed wire fence. At last he made it.

The fox went bounding off across the field. The bright orange fur rose and fell, rose and fell, making arcs above the bright green alfalfa. I watched spellbound until he was only a wisp threading through the distant grass. Meanwhile Uncle Thurman and Woodsie had jumped out to see about the White Leghorn fryer the fox had left behind. It had sustained considerable damage about the neck, and it was wobbling and squawking. Gladys made Thurman go up to the house and try to return the chicken to its rightful owners, but no one answered the door.

Woodsie began to laugh and said, "Well, there's only one thing to do now." She headed for the chicken.

Gladys shrilly objected, "You can't take that chicken! That's stealing! It belongs to the people who live over there."

Woodsie just giggled. It had been nearly half an hour since we had seen another automobile, so my five-foot grandmother scooped up the chicken, walked onto the two-lane highway, and planted her feet wide apart in the middle of the road. Still laughing, she stood there and wrung that chicken's neck. All the while, from her mountain of pillows in the front seat of the Ford, Gladys squealed, "Mother,

Mother, somebody'll *see you!*" I looked in all directions across that level place. I was sure there was not another soul anywhere in all the miles between my funny little grandmother and the distant mountains.

The chicken was wrapped in newspaper, and when we got back to Balmorhea we had fried chicken for supper. But Aunt Gladys refused to eat any because it was a *stolen* chicken.

That fall Uncle Thurman asked to be transferred to a city where there was a major medical center. My Aunt Gladys died the next summer, and my kind uncle, who was an odd sort of fellow, became quieter and even harder to figure out than before. If Woodsie grieved, she did so in private. Whenever I was around, she was her regular, funny old playful self.

Now when I think of far West Texas, I remember that summer of my childhood with its mystery trips. I see a red fox escaping through a field of alfalfa and an oval bed of rose quartz crystals, shimmering pink. Again and again in memory, the four of us walk single file—my grandmother, my aunt and uncle, and me—past the white ribs of a wild mustang lying in the clear water of Phantom Lake.

The Stonemason

My tough old Scottish forefathers were among the first white settlers in the mountains of western North Carolina, where they did their best to keep their culture alive. The families of stonecutters handed down their craft, and in time they held Highland games and hollering contests. My own family—the Taylors—continues to pass on its peculiarly Scottish values, generation after generation.

It shouldn't be a surprise, then, that I had a strictly no-nonsense upbringing. My parents were plainspoken people. Blunt, in fact. They expected a lot from their children but didn't waste compliments. They didn't waste *anything.* We never lacked for essentials, but there were few frills. Even Santa Claus brought practical gifts. We certainly didn't do things just to impress the neighbors. I couldn't remember one single thing my family had ever done that could be called extravagant. Then I went to a high school class reunion.

After the banquet, a group of us gathered at a friend's house and talked far into the night. Three or four of us had been classmates from the first grade all the way through high school, and we talked about how that little town looked when we were small. We talked about our perceptions of the people we had known, and because we were remembering the time of the Great Depression, we talked about our perceptions of wealth.

Now, children tend to think of wealth as the ownership of whatever they wish they had. I mentioned to my friend Anne how I had always thought her family must be rich because they took real vacations—not just trips to visit relatives. Even during the Depression, they traveled to exotic destinations: Galveston, Carlsbad Caverns, Pike's Peak! We talked about how impressed we were with one family in town who had their name carved into the cornerstone of a stone building down on the square. I turned to my friend Margaret who, like me, had been a skinny girl but who, like me, was skinny no more, and said, "Oh, we thought you were something because there was a street named for your family." She laughed. "You do know, don't you, that it wasn't our dirt-poor generation who had the street named after us! And by the way, that street is still only four blocks long. And in the wrong part of town."

Someone said to Stella how envious we had been of her. She wore ready-made clothes. Her parents owned Kirtley's dress shop, and her mother bought her dresses at wholesale twice a year when she went to market. Then someone—it may have been Nadine Randall—whirled around in my direction and said, "But Rosy, your family showed us what it meant to be truly wealthy." I stared. I couldn't think of anything to say. Our family didn't do extravagant things.

I protested, "What on earth gave you that idea?" Someone said, "Well, you lived in a two-story house." Someone else chimed in, "And you had all those big shade trees in your yard." I thought, "Oh, that explains it." To a West Texas child in the days of the Dust Bowl, trees meant you were wealthy. But they went on. They liked coming to our house because they loved our fishpond and all the beautiful stonework around our yard.

And I thought, "You're right . . ." I had always just accepted all that stonework and that fishpond. But they were right. We didn't do extravagant things, and yet there was that elaborate fishpond. It certainly wasn't a necessity.

You see, in mid-Depression, our family bought a new house. Actually, it really wasn't a *new* house. It was, in fact, a very old house, and the elders in town referred to it as "the old Dr. Hamilton place." That house had fallen on hard times. Before we could even move into it, a lot of work had to be done inside and out. The floors were sanded and refinished. The walls with their loose canvas and wallpaper were stripped, sheet-rocked, and repapered. The woodwork and cabinetry and the bathrooms were redone. Then a man came with a team of mules. He plowed up that long-neglected yard and planted grass for lawns. And the whole family went out together to plant a vegetable garden and a strawberry patch. Those strawberries were as close to an extravagance as I could remember in my young life.

Then one morning, because I was the only one not old enough to go to school, I watched as a dilapidated flatbed truck pulled into the driveway. A man got out. I recognized his face from Sundays at church. He brought down off the truck a big bundle of short stakes, a level, a tape measure, and a hefty ball of bright yellow twine. He began to drive stakes and to stretch yellow cord all along the perimeter of our yard. Yellow string went from the porch to the curb and along the driveway, all the way back to the old carriage house. By the end of the day our side yard had become a maze of string. When I asked him what he was doing, he said, "Why don't you just watch and see if you can guess. But please don't step on the yellow cord."

The next day the man was back, and he began to dig in our side yard. He scooped out a huge, deep hole. He built wooden forms and poured concrete. And gradually there emerged a beautiful, ground-level fishpond. He faced the pond all around with a wide stone walkway. And he just kept building.

He built some of the most beautiful stone walkways I've ever seen. I was fascinated, and I must have been a real pest because I asked him a million questions. I watched while those rough hands worked quickly, expertly, with the stone. He cut the stone and fit the pieces neatly into place. He tapped the stone, and it broke exactly where he wanted it to break. I asked him how he knew how to do that. He said, "You have to *respect* the stone and work with it." But what did that mean?

He smoothed the mortar and filed off the sharp edges. He didn't seem surprised when I asked him, "Why are you doing that?" He said he didn't want me to stub my toes or skin my knees.

"As a matter of fact," he said, "I don't want *your* children to stub their toes here, either."

I said, "I don't have any children. I'm only *five!*"

He laughed, "Oh, but you will, and they'll come here to play, too."

My children. An extraordinary thought to a five-year-old. "Fine stonework," he said, "lasts forever." I didn't know how long "forever" was, but if it included my children, I thought it was going to be a long time coming.

That beautiful fishpond was filled, and water lilies were planted in the corners. There was a tiny bubbling fountain in the middle, and an elaborate drainage system so it could be emptied easily for cleaning. And then the pond was stocked with big, fan-tailed fish. Some were white with black spots, others were a deep orange, and some were jet black with long flowing tails.

My friends and I spent many hours there, feeding bread or stale crackers to the goldfish or just watching them. We played jacks and hopscotch on the stone walkways. And when we were thirteen, Teddy McNeil tried to jump across the fishpond and fell in.

As I grew up, I became more aware of that stonemason and of his friendship with my father. Their connection was puzzling to me. He was not one of those men who hunted or played chess with my dad. He and his wife were not among the couples who played 42 on Friday nights. They were not part of that group of friends who bought tickets to ball games together or came out to the lake house for weekends. There was a different kind of bond between my father and the stonemason.

As my father's health began to fail, there were some Sunday

mornings when he was not well enough to be in Sunday school and church. On those afternoons, our doorbell would ring, and one of my parents would say, "I expect I know who that is." There at the front door would stand the stonemason and his wife, usually holding a little plate of cookies or a pie, or some other treat. They stopped by for just a few minutes to check on my dad, and to see if he needed anything.

Over the next twenty years or so, as my father's illness grew steadily worse, there were many long and frightening hospital stays. I came to know and expect that anytime my father was at Memorial, I would see the stonemason. Late in the evening, after a long day's work, he would appear quietly at the door of the hospital room, his thinning hair still wet from the shower, combed down neatly in place. He would be wearing the trousers to his Sunday suit, a fresh white shirt, and a tie. Those rough hands, bleached a grayish white from years and years of mortar dust, would be scrubbed almost to bleeding. And he would say to my mother or whoever was there, "Honey, you go on home and rest. I'll sit the night with Dick." And many, many nights he did that. We knew that it was safe for us to leave because he was there.

During one really precarious time, the family called and told me I'd better get in the car and come quickly. I arrived expecting to find the house deserted and everyone at the hospital. I pulled into the driveway behind a tired-looking brown truck. As I took my bag from the trunk, some motion caught my eye, and I turned to look up to the second floor. There was the stonemason, wearing a little carpenter's apron, tapping away at the upper porch railing. I called out, "Hi, Carl. What are you doing up there?" He just grinned and waved and said, "Hi, honey. I'm glad you're here. I came by here to check on your dad a week or two ago and saw this railing was loose. Thought I'd just come by today and fix it. I knew I'd just be in the way down at the hospital. Didn't know what else to do."

When my dad was well enough to come home, he walked with difficulty from the car into the house. He looked up and said, "Who fixed the railing?" And I answered, "Carl came by and did that." He shook his head and said softly, "I should have known."

About that time my husband and I had bought a house in a new subdivision, a little brick number much like its neighbors all down the street. And we began to put in a yard for our children to play in. As we planned the landscaping, I kept looking around that yard, feeling that something was missing. Finally I said, "You know, I think somehow it might feel more like home if it had a bit of stonework." Soon I was lugging home books about landscaping with stone, and I began to read. Rather timidly, I built stone borders around my flower beds. Then with a little more skill and a lot more courage, we began to construct a retaining wall at the base of the sloping back yard. As we worked, I thought a lot about Carl. I thought about all the beautiful masonry he'd done at my parents' home, especially the fishpond. And as we pieced together our stone jigsaw puzzle, more and more I came to appreciate that man's expertise.

Shortly after we finished the retaining wall along the back of our little house, my sister and her husband both came down with pneumonia, and my mother went to take care of the children. By then my father's health was much too fragile for him to be left alone, so we brought him to our house for a couple of months. I did my best to keep him entertained. I got him to help me label some snapshots and some old family photographs. I asked him to talk about our family history and took some notes. I encouraged him to tell some of my favorite stories, just so I could hear them again. And I cooked all of his favorite foods to fatten him up a little bit. But my children seemed to hold his interest best of all.

One morning as I was doing the breakfast dishes, I looked out the window. My father was standing in the back yard, sizing up my retaining wall with a rather amused expression. I picked up my coffee cup and went out to join him. "What do you think about my stonework, Dad?" He looked it over another minute and said, "You know, that's not a bad job for your first project." Generous praise from an old Scotsman.

I got him settled in a recliner over on the terrace and sat down nearby to talk. The children played not far away. I said, "Dad, I don't know that I ever told you how much I enjoyed that stonework at home." He smiled and said, "Well, I'm glad." I continued, "You know, those walkways made me a V.I.P. in the neighborhood. I was the only kid who could play hopscotch without having to get out a piece of chalk and draw a court. Those stone walks made a permanent, ready-made hopscotch court." He chuckled. Next I said, "And I really loved the fishpond."

My little girl came over and leaned against the arm of his chair. "Grandpa, I like your fishpond, too. I like feeding crackers to the fish." And as I listened, I was thinking, *My children had come there to play* . . . She went on, "We asked Mom if she'd build us a fishpond, but she said we didn't have room. She said if *she* built one, it'd probably leak." We laughed. "Dad," I said, "while I worked on this retaining wall I really started to appreciate the quality of all that rockwork at your house. I know now it must have been a terribly expensive thing to do in mid-Depression." He avoided my eyes and looked a little embarrassed. "Oh, not really." But I wanted to know. "Why did you decide to have all those walkways built, and that elaborate pond? It seems like such an extravagance." He stared at my beginner's stonework, then off into the distance, and cleared his throat. I knew those signs. They meant I was about to hear a story of some significance.

There was a long, long silence. I was prepared to wait him out. He looked down at his hands and seemed to be struggling. At last he began, almost in a whisper, "Well, you know, back during the Depression things were pretty hard. I knew a good man. . . . The bank wouldn't make him a loan, and I loaned him some money so he could stay in business. He kept worrying because he couldn't pay me back. So finally I thought up that project so I could write off the loan, and he could call it paid. I really just wanted him to forget about it."

After another long pause my father said, "You know, I don't think he ever has . . . forgotten about it." And I was thinking, "Of course."

Questions answered. Mystery solved. Now I understood all those nights at the hospital and all those Sunday afternoon cookies. I wondered, "Should I tell him that I remember watching the mason lay all that stone, and that I know the man he's talking about?" My father had carefully avoided mentioning the man's name.

For once I held my tongue. I was thinking, "I'll let you keep your very private transaction to yourself, and I'll keep my part of the secret, too."

But you know, my friends at the class reunion were right. That fishpond was a symbol of what it means to be truly wealthy. It's just that they were thinking of the kind of wealth that fills your pocket, and now I understand that fishpond was a sign of the wealth of friendship. Like fine stonework. The kind that lasts forever.